THE
LORAN

A LANCE GEDRIN MYSTERY

GREG
GOUNTANIS

RB
ROWDY BOOKS

Published by Rowdy Books

Ebook ISBN: 978-1-953762-05-4

Paperback ISBN: 978-1-953762-04-7

Cover design by Deranged Doctor Design

First edition: July 2021

For Max

1

I'm a hooker. When carbon steel collides with the urethane sphere in front of my feet, sidespin rules the roost. Thousands of RPMs taunt me as the white dimples take off opposite their intended line. A hooker can make a variety of changes: grip, ball position, stance, weight at address. But at the end of the day, it all means shit.

Golf is a Jekyll and Hyde game.

One minute you're king, and the next you're that kid who fucks up the word "received" at the spelling bee. Mechanics are the real deal, and the fine details make or break the game. One degree variance in club face position at impact meant your shot would fly two yards off line.

The average amateur is off several degrees.

I learned all this as a sophomore in high school, carrying a bag of wooden brassies around the links. I'd take in the luscious greens, the slanting tee boxes, the slippery bunkers, and I'd hack my ball around the slopes. I'd keep score in my head, and I quickly learned that a professor was required to play the game at a high level. Study the angles and the centrifugal forces and there was a sliver of hope you'd make a name for yourself.

So while the other kiddos would boast about getting laid and swiping whiskey from their parents' lake house, I'd boast about nailing slick six-footers downhill with a left-to-right break. I'd rave about the nuances of bent grass greens and blue-grass and Poa annua. Stimpmeter was my middle name, and five-hour rounds were bliss.

But all good things come to their natural end.

In my case, I realized that my true talents lay elsewhere. I couldn't eagle a damned hole, but the moment I stepped foot in Sal's boxing gym I was walking on air. Fully approved warfare. Blood, sweat, and tears. Pure, unabashed chaos. I donned the gloves, and the first time I sparred I bashed somebody's brains in. Nobody could touch me.

So I traded in my clubs and I never looked back. I rose up the ranks faster than you could say *hola*. Every promoter wanted me on their card, and it wasn't long before I became the undisputed heavyweight champ. I would have kept my title, too, if it wasn't for the fact that I was wrongfully convicted of murder. Twelve years in the slammer before I was sprung by my lawyer, who was moonlighting as a serial killer—literally.

Such is life.

Now, I don't bring all this up for pity points. I call balls and strikes better than anybody. I bring all this up because it's fucking obvious that you can't improve your swing in a seven-by-eleven cell with zero equipment and a bunch of hombres trying to shank you after hours. Which explains why my first round of golf in roughly two decades was no bueno.

I stood now on the eighteenth tee at Rainmaker Golf Club in Alto, New Mexico. Freedom is a beautiful thing. I'd wanted to get back out there and see if muscle memory was real. The sun peeked out over the canyons, and when the clouds parted, the ambience was something straight out of a magazine. My agent, Mark Sims, had pulled some strings and gotten me a tee time right at civil twilight. I'd started the round with a glow-in-the-dark golf ball and plenty of shitty swings, but my game steadily improved on the front nine, and I was on pace now to shoot even par on the back.

If I parred eighteen.

I analyzed the hole and knew that it called for a cut. It was a dogleg right par five. I was playing from the middle tees, and there was no chance in hell I'd be able to reach in two shots. Hell, I'd reached a par five in two just once in my golfing life, and that was because a seagull played favorites one time, picked up my ball, and dropped it on the green. I'd proceeded to four-putt that hole. The course giveth and the course taketh away.

There were no seagulls in sight today. This hole would need three good swings to get on the green. The problem with being a hooker was that while the ball did end up getting more carry than it would with a fade, the ball also had much more sidespin, and sailed out of bounds quite frequently. So I pictured a fade and made what I thought was a fade swing, a little more out-to-in than in-to-out through impact. I hooked anyway, my ball snagging the left rough, but I was in play.

And Henri took off.

The rascal didn't understand that caddies needed to exercise a great degree of decorum on such fine courses. Repair ball marks. Fix divots. Rake bunkers. Wipe the residue off of the clubs. Henri, by contrast, had a tendency to bark at the elk and chase down the stray snakes. But I was a clever owner, and a clever owner assimilates to the situation and uses it as a teaching moment. Each ball that I hit, and that Henri retrieved, merited one treat. If Henri left my ball in its original spot, that merited two treats. Henri was a quick study. After the first few slobber balls, Henri realized that if he simply stopped beside my ball and ceased his slobbering ways, he'd get not only two treats, but two very fancy ones. Out with the chicken and in with the venison. I knew how to play it, and Henri and I had been on the same page for most of the round. He was loving every second of it, and I was loving his companionship. A dog is man's best friend for a reason.

This time, Henri found my ball in twenty seconds. I took about twenty-five seconds with my cart. When I reached my ball, I looked at Henri, then back at my ball, then at the lie, then the flag, then at Henri again. If he was flustered, he didn't show it. He sat with his chest out and ears perked up, analyzing every sound known to man around him. He eventually gave up the act and started begging. I stared him down for a few seconds, and he went quiet. We were at a standstill. Then he held out his paw like a good citizen, and I took it.

"Good boy," I said.

Can't go wrong with venison. I handed him two more treats.

I had about three hundred and seven yards to the pin. Golf was the quintessential chess match. Position your ball at the right angles and quadrants, and you have a shot at shooting your best score. I wanted to lay up on the right side of the fairway, about one hundred fifty yards out. That would give me another one-hundred-fifty-yard shot to the green. Based on my ball striking today, that was a smooth seven iron. I took a couple practice swings and gave up my hooker card, at least for one shot. The ball faded this time, right to my landing spot.

Henri took off, and the process started again. Find ball. Drive cart. Staring contest. Give treat. Play on. When the round was over perhaps I'd go into the clubhouse and get some souvenirs for the road, to remember the place. Ever since I'd gotten out of Pontiac Correctional, I'd been the quintessential nomad. No car. No fixed address. No obligations. I'd gone from

Chicago to Oregon to Vegas to New Mexico, always with Henri by my side. I didn't feel comfortable in any one spot. And besides, I lived by my rules.

I had so much left to do with my second chance at life. When you come within seconds of receiving a government-sanctioned three-drug cocktail that will stop your heart forever, things become crystal clear. Next on the bucket list was Old Faithful in Yellowstone. Henri would get a kick out of the geothermal feature. Of course, this was all after I gave my speech tonight at Dobermans for Life. When word got out about how I'd rescued Henri, and the many talents he had developed on the trail, the society felt I'd be the perfect keynote speaker. I never turned down a good speech, and I'd accepted faster than a cheetah on the prowl.

But first, one more solid shot to go on eighteen. You're only as good as your next shot.

I surveyed the pin. It was tucked in the back left of the green, a few paces off the edge. A draw would get me there, but leave me with a big-ass sloping uphill putt. The safe play would be to hit to the fat part of the green, take my two putts, and call it a day. Even par for the back and that'd be all she wrote. The aggressive play would be to fly the ball right over the flag and have it check. If played absolutely perfectly, it'd check, hit the slope, and funnel back toward the hole.

Gravity.

I smiled and made the aggressive play. I took a nice divot, and dammit, I hit the perfect shot. My ball launched twenty degrees in the air and started drawing toward the flag. It landed two feet over the flag and checked. Then it started rolling down, closer and closer to perfection.

But then everything changed.

The ball hit something on the green and spun left. I still had a ten-footer for birdie, but I could have had a tap-in.

Henri was tired this time and hitched a ride in my cart. I drove all the way up to the cart path left of the green, parked, took my putter out, and walked to the obstruction that had messed with my shot. Normally I'd mark my ball, swat the obstruction aside, and get back to my putt.

Not now.

I froze.

The obstruction was a vintage Lord Marvel Seiko watch with the initials "R.S." engraved on the side of the crown.

It was my dad's watch.

The very same watch I'd seen buried at my mom's funeral.

2

I never met my dad. Papa Gedrin, aka Ronnie Spikes, was an Alaskan crab fisherman who loved the sweatiest jobs and salivated over the deadliest catches. He'd flash his pearly whites, swing those nets over the concrete slabs he had for shoulders, and negotiate a bunch of moolah for his trials and tribulations.

He'd stop in town after town and break bread with the locals. They'd look at him with wary, drunken eyes and broken teeth, and he'd regale them with his exploits on the high seas. Some would give him a few pints on the house for his tales, while others would give him the evil eye. Papa Gedrin had a tendency to distract all the ladies from their men, and he'd direct his yarns accordingly, making eye contact at all the right times. He'd laugh and smile and put a hand on their shoulders and pronounce their names incorrectly just to get a reaction. He had a script, and he'd memorized it to a tee.

But in Seward, Alaska, on a blistery fall night, he quit the act and bought Mama Gedrin a cherry cocktail at the bar. The rest is history.

That's how Mama Gedrin described it to me growing up. I came into this world eleven months and seven days after that cocktail. Part crab fisherman, part teacher, part miscreant.

The Gedrin blood.

I ran the watch in my hands now, feeling for any imperfections on the straps. There were many, meaning this wasn't some newbie replica of my dad's timepiece. This was the real deal. I flipped it over a couple more times, then I put it aside.

I had unfinished business.

I lined up my birdie putt. It was half a cup outside the right edge. I looked at my ball, then the hole, then my ball again. I stroked the putt smoothly, but missed it badly. The ball hit the left edge and rolled back toward my feet. I jumped out of the way, and the vibration caused the ball to pick up speed down the slope. It stopped twelve feet away, with even more of an uphill break for par. Henri was silent, but he should have complained. I shook my head, re-gripped my putter, gritted my teeth, and then nailed it, dead center of the cup. Sometimes anger is the antidote on the links.

Even par on the back nine. Eighty-seven for the day. Not bad for an old high school kid.

I went back to the watch. While Papa Gedrin loved the crabs, there was one thing he might have loved even more. Bling. He'd wooed my mom with jewels and purses and rings and necklaces when they dated. He'd been the best of the best on the seas, I guess. But there was one piece that had never left his side: the Lord Marvel Seiko 36,000. It was sleek, with a manual wind movement, silver dial, and brush finish. The thing was classic in every sense of the word and probably still retailed for close to five hundred bucks. Classic meant character which meant clout which meant you were the shit.

I didn't need to conjure up any more stories my mom told me about my dad. All the pics in our house were a walking billboard for the man and his timepiece. Watch on the beach. Watch at the ball game. Watch on the dock. Watch in the gym. Truth be told, it was a damned shrine.

The only reason my dad ever parted with the piece was because he'd left it at her place by accident and died on the job. A wave threw him overboard and that's all she wrote. Mama Gedrin got the word back from some of his crewmates. I was an infant at the time and didn't remember shit. Growing up, Mom would always say she wanted to get buried with that watch for old times' sake. And she kept true to her word. When she left this earth, that watch was placed in her hands as her casket was lowered into the earth for eternity. An homage to her crab fisherman.

I'd seen the whole thing. I was still in Pontiac at the time, but I'd been granted a furlough from the Illinois Department of Corrections for bereavement purposes. Escorted, of course. Bottom line, my eyes didn't lie. The watch was buried with Mom.

Now, it was here in New Mexico.

Who did it, and why on the eighteenth green at Rainmaker? I asked Henri, but he was too busy barking at the elk again to care. I analyzed the watch's leather one more time. Solid brown alligator leather with small rivulets, worn down by untold hours of perspiration. The dial had a few scuffs, but nothing remarkable. The crown had some grass on it, and the bezel had specks of sand caked around the side—perhaps the culprit dropped it in the bunker before placing it on the green.

A simple mind would say there could easily be hundreds of vintage Seikos traipsing around the world. One click and it's in your hands a couple days later with free shipping to boot. Used watches are still the shit. But my synapses weren't simple, and I didn't believe in coincidences. Somebody was sending me a message about my dad, Ronnie Spikes.

I heard it loud and clear, and now I was gonna get to the bottom of it.

I walked back to my cart and noticed a greenskeeper watering a hole a few paces off the cart path.

"You lose a watch?" I said.

The greenskeeper stared down at the hole, oblivious to the world around him. He had a weathered, sunburnt look that said he'd been around these fairways for far too long to truly care about them. He was as vintage as the Seiko.

I took a few steps closer, and the greenskeeper looked up.

"Your watch?" I repeated.

He looked at me, then at the watch, then shook his head.

"Nie, mow," he said.

I knew English, Spanish, and a smidge of Swahili, but I couldn't speak a lick of Polish. I knew those were Polish words from some of the hombres in the fight game.

Nie, mow. *I don't speak.* English, presumably. The greenskeeper was warding off the unknown, and I didn't blame him.

I tried a different tack. I pointed to the watch and held it up in front of his eyes, like I was gonna hypnotize him. The greenskeeper took a long hard look at it, then went back to the hole in the ground. It wasn't just any hole, but a turtle's nest, so I had to give the keeper some props. He had his work cut out for him, protecting life in that nest amongst the throng of errant tee shots that could destroy it all in a heartbeat. Imagine explaining that to your English-speaking boss. Hell, even Henri was a threat. He sniffed at the edge of the nest, inspecting.

I snapped my fingers and Henri ran back to the cart. He was the top service animal in town, bar none.

I bid the keeper adieu, got back in my cart, and drove to the pro shop. Henri's energy was back, so he sprinted alongside the cart the whole way there. I parked and told Henri to wait.

When he sat, I tossed him another piece of venison. Then I went in.

Shopping was one of my favorite activities when I had the time, the desire, and the dinero. The former had never been an issue, but the latter had been an impediment for quite some time. Pontiac didn't exactly lend itself to a high net worth. But the world works itself out. I eventually went back to bashing brains for profit, and dinero was no longer a concern, with contracts rolling in and Sims working his magic with random endorsements. Since I'd gotten out, I'd worn a green tent sombrero, some funky purple socks, and I'd donned some deodorant that started with the letter "Q." The suits loved every minute of it, and I loved messing with them in all the commercials. I'd kept my affiliation with pancakes intact and had worn my famous "I Love Maple Syrup" shirt in every spot, mashing the product displays.

My way or the highway, hombre.

But this time I didn't want items. I wanted answers. About the watch.

I waited in line, and when it was my turn I said, "Who's in charge of your lost and found?"

A pimply boy in braces smiled. "Sir, that'd be me. Are you the putter guy? This is one fine Odyssey."

He pulled a putter out from behind the counter.

"I missed my birdie, junior. That putter ain't mine," I said.

"Sorry, sir. Some dude's been losing his putter every round on this course. Keeps coming back, losing it on twelve, finding it. Repeat. We should glue the damned thing to his cart."

"Gorilla Glue works wonders," I said. I held up the Seiko, and the boy looked puzzled.

"Sir?" he said.

"Who played the last round here, yesterday?"

I figured if the watch wasn't the keeper's, it was whoever

11

the hell had finished up their round last night. I was the first tee time this morning, and all the groups started on hole one.

"Sir, that's private."

"National security, junior?"

The boy's face turned red. "No, but it's privacy and shit. I don't want to get in trouble."

"Look my name up in the system, right quick." Everything was computerized these days. Apps. Maps. Tee times.

The boy played along and looked me up. Then his eyes widened like he'd seen a million ghosts. I hated to play the Gedrin card, but hell, when you have the game to play it, why not?

"Mr. G-Gedrin," he stammered. "Wow, I hope you've had a great time playing today. I can book you for the same time tomorrow if you like, no charge."

"That won't be necessary, kiddo. Who played?"

The braces boy looked both ways, as if hiding from imaginary Gestapo. Then he turned back toward me.

"Paco Macho," he said.

It had a nice ring to it.

I thanked the boy for his hospitality and walked out. Henri was in the cart again, ready for another round. But I was ready to find Macho.

I took out my Jitterbug and concluded my research in three minutes flat. Sims had given me an unlimited plan, and I wasn't that much of a dinosaur anymore.

From the looks of it, Macho got out on the links often, and with some very big players.

He was about to meet the biggest player of them all.

Me.

3

Macho also got high on rubber. He'd started in the bowels of the auto bays, doing transmissions and oil changes, and then he'd graduated to tires and performance-enhancing rims. He'd plaster fancy decals all over the hoods and bumpers, and he'd pimp those rides faster and cheaper than anybody in town.

Yet his claim to fame began with something far simpler: a run-of-the-mill tire rotation for thirty-nine bucks. On the day he made a name for himself, Macho wore blue overalls and had a flashlight taped to his head. He cracked jokes with the rest of the dudes in the auto bay as he narrated the tire rotation process every step of the way, adding a bunch of flair to a very simple task. One of those dudes happened to be recording.

"We eat flats for breakfast at Paco's Tires," Macho said in the video, taking a flat tire and chewing a piece of rubber. He repeated the phrase seven times, each time chewing more and more of those flats. When it was all said and done, he was rushed to the hospital for his rubber-eating exploits. But the video went viral.

Macho made the cover of *Motor Trend* and appeared on CNN and all the local channels. And he never looked back. He used the money from his hit video to open up his first tire shop in Albuquerque, New Mexico. Being an employee just wasn't cool enough anymore. Everywhere he went he was recognized as the flats guy, and his celebrity led to three tire shops, then five, and then so many a mathematician couldn't count them right.

Macho was new money. He was the tire don, and no competitor could hold his lunch basket. He ran the New Mexico tire game, and judging from his exploits he had a seat at the table with the governor of New Mexico, the mayor of Albuquerque, and more. Macho had all the connects, and he'd sure as hell worked them on the golf course.

The Jitterbug didn't lie. I flipped through photos of Macho on my phone, analyzing the dude's body language. He seemed like pure shyster, but people like that sizzle. The biggest showmen get the bacon, and that was something that had gone on from the beginning of time and would sure as hell go on till the end of time.

I closed my browser, and Henri and I stepped out of our Uber at Macho's shop. One of them anyway. Henri sniffed around the perimeter, but didn't slobber or piss anywhere. He was becoming a better citizen each day.

My plan was to find Macho and ask him a question. Then he'd give me an answer, and I'd ask him another question. We'd take turns till one of us got tired or the other fessed up. That's how I rolled in the amateur sleuth game. I could roll with the punches, but I could also take the bull by the horns if the situation called for it. I was great at improv and would have made a great thespian if it weren't for my brain-bashing skills.

I didn't see anybody at the front entrance to the shop, but I saw plenty of people in the auto bays. The place had four bays, and each was about twenty feet long and forty feet wide. Being at the top of the heap was real. Macho could work on school buses in those bays if he wanted to. There were no buses today though—just two luxury sedans, a station wagon, and a pickup truck with so much dust on it I wondered if it had come right out of the Sahara.

Henri couldn't get enough of the new smells. He ran from bay to bay, wagging his tail like a boss and getting some sprints in. A few of the workers smiled, a few of them frowned, and a few of them sat huddled at a corner table eating from their lunchboxes. I wanted to give them a proper show, so I told Henri to "roll over," "bark," "paw," and "play dead." He performed flawlessly, and the masses were thoroughly impressed.

I would have given him more commands, but somebody spoiled the party.

"Employees only, asshole," a voice said.

I turned and saw an inked-up brunette, with a plethora of piercings. I was impervious to body art from my time on the inside, to the point where if I *didn't* see body art I thought they were fucked up. Normal peeps had body art, right? Like this brunette. Her art was quite simply muy bueno. I was turned on, and this was usually a recipe for disaster.

I bit my tongue. The brunette before me was a solid five-nine and one hundred thirty pounds of model bliss. Her curves ran for miles, and the infamous hourglass had her name on it. Her eyes had soft, grayish hues that belied her grit working among the boys. She didn't play.

I wanted to continue my interaction with her, but my track record with the female sex was the worst parabola of all time. Just when I thought I'd understood the modern-day woman, the mundo would put me in my place. Time after time. But luckily for me, I had so few brain cells left that I went into each encounter expecting a turn of the tide. Success was right around the corner, hombre. Maybe this shop gal would eternally lower my blood pressure.

Time would tell.

"I eat flats for breakfast," I said.

The brunette frowned. "Wise guy, sign in and wait for your car to get serviced like everyone else."

"I came to see Macho," I said.

"Who?"

"Your jefe."

The brunette still didn't understand, so I pointed to a picture above one of the bays showing Macho smiling with his handlebar mustache, cowboy boots, and ginormous belly. By the looks of it, the jefe had put on the freshman fifteen quite a few times since his viral hit.

"We're all looking for him," she said. "Till then Rachel Hattie runs the show here, and I say get the hell back to the lobby like everybody else."

I smiled. "Challenge accepted."

I stood my ground like Henri did for that venison.

Hattie was flustered by my response. I could see the gears churning in her head, probably trying to figure out how to dispel me from her domain. She furrowed her brows, closed her eyes, and for a moment I thought I was gonna get shanked.

Then she came out of it, the humorous Hattie.

"You're such a trip," she said. "That work at the shop down the street?"

"I have many carefully crafted tactics," I said. "Ready to unleash on unsuspecting gals in the auto bay. Now, where's Macho?"

"He's out being Macho?"

"Rich."

"He wipes his ass with hundreds, the devil." Hattie

grinned, and I knew right there that our interaction would indeed last far longer and far wider than in this auto bay. I didn't play.

"Shame, I wipe with those dollar coins. Less residue."

Hattie shook her head. "Back to the service area, man. You're done."

"I need to ask Macho a very important question." I gave Hattie a look that said my question was really damned important.

Hattie mulled it over for a few seconds. She looked around the bay, taking note of the workers and the cars in the shop. Then she caved.

"He didn't come in this morning," she said. "You'll have to wait to ask him whatever the hell you wanna ask him."

"What time's his shift?" I asked.

"Dawn to dusk."

"Maybe he's at one of the other shops? A million of them, right? I can catch him there."

Hattie shook her head. "This is the flagship shop. This is where it all started. He sends runners to the other shops to report back to him. He's never missed a day here."

"Call him," I said.

"He never answers his phone in the mornings. He's kind of old school like that." Hattie rolled her eyes.

"A man not beholden to technology is quite a man indeed," I said.

"Doubtful. He's an asshole and doesn't want more bad press. If you hide from it, it's not real."

"Those flats did a number on him."

Hattie laughed, and I did too.

"Where's your car?" Hattie said. "We can put it in bay one next."

"I refuse to make payments on a depreciating asset," I said.

Hattie raised her eyebrows like she'd just heard a crackpot theory on how the world is flat.

I kept sleuthing.

"Maybe Macho had a series of odd but easily explainable events this morning," I said.

"Preach."

Before I could say more, I got mobbed.

4

A worker with a red bandana and Jesus necklace wanted my autograph. "Gedrin, you kicked Juko's ass. He ain't got shit on you."

He held out a smudgy legal pad with a ballpoint pen.

I smiled for the imaginary cameras and gave my John Hancock. It was one of my better acts of penmanship. Clean lines and swoops, followed by a personalized message to the recipient. *Eat those flats, dude,* I wrote.

The worker looked like a million bucks, but where there's smoke, there's fire. The rest of his compadres flooded me with various objects for me to sign. I had no objection. Hell, before the fall I'd signed on people's tibias, elbows, knees, and the occasional pair of double D's. A professional autographer never judges his seeker.

I wrote different messages for the compadres, but eventually Henri had had enough of my penmanship. He growled and chased them away.

And it was back to me and Hattie in a pungent auto bay somewhere in New Mexico.

If she was shocked by my celeb ways, she didn't show it. She walked over to one of the auto bays and examined the station wagon. She gazed at every crevice like she was about to prep for brain surgery, then she grabbed a clipboard next to one of the work benches and scribbled something. When she was satisfied, she pulled a wrench out of a box and went back to the station wagon.

"A somebody in my shop," she said. "Imagine that."

She started fixing the station wagon. The compadres apparently weren't up to par.

"The world is strange indeed," I said.

"How long have you been in the game?"

"Long enough to know it's been a tad bit too long."

"Shame. I like them fighting boys." Hattie picked the clipboard back up and scribbled again. She shook her head like she was giving a bad report card. Then she put the wrench back in the box. If it wasn't for Henri chasing the workers away, she'd probably have ripped them a new one for their struggles.

Everything happens for a reason.

I smiled. "There's not an ounce of boy anywhere up in here."

I held her gaze, and she looked away. She was blushing slightly, and I knew I was on the right track. Gaining rapport was seldom an easy task, but once you got the telltale signs of interest, the tables would turn. I was chillin' like a villain. For now. We stood there for a minute taking in the tools and the metallics and Macho's belly on the wall.

Then Hattie made the next move.

"Come on over," she said.

She led me to her office and pointed to a dilapidated armchair with purple fuzz all over it. She sat on her side and I sat on mine. Her chair was black high-back leather, probably seven years old minimum. It was broken in nicely and looked quite comfortable. I couldn't say the same about her desk. Mounds of receipts and staples and miscellaneous parts covered every inch of it, and her computer looked like it had been in its prime years before my wrongful incarceration.

"Macho has excellent decor," I said.

Hattie cleared some space on the desk, but it was futile. The papers flooded back into the same spot. She pulled out a water bottle and took a swig.

Then she glanced over my right shoulder. Henri sat in the entryway, wagging his tail.

"What's his deal?" she said.

"A service companion always waits for his owner to inspect the premises, then give the go-ahead. An owner must throw himself in the line of fire for the betterment of his canine pal."

"Sure looked like he was in that line of fire inspecting those bays before you waltzed on in here."

"I scoped the place out from the comfort of an Uber, faster than you can say Uber."

Hattie smiled. "What's your infirmity, carless wonder?"

"Which one? I have mucho."

"The one that got you the dog."

I told Henri "come" and he came in and heeled on my left side, tongue out. I gave him a treat, sans venison, and rubbed his whiskers. Henri lay down on all fours and smiled.

"Missy, my infirmity is between the ears." I pointed to my brain and tapped it with my index finger.

Hattie shook her head. "You're gaming the system just like my dad did. Sooner or later it'll catch up to you, man. My dad got charged with fraud. Just saying. You've got the whole boxing thing, but I wouldn't get too comfortable."

I stood up from my chair and did a little dance, just to mess with her. Then I pulled out a scraggly piece of paper from my jeans pocket.

"I got doctor's notes and the whole nine yards. My brain cells are like flimsy french fries. Some days I wonder how I can beat people's brains in that ring so easily. Other days I forget simple tasks."

"Like what?"

"Like what color biscuit I just gave Henri. I switch up the colors on him constantly. Different taste, different texture. But sometimes the patterns elude me."

"You didn't give him a biscuit," Hattie said.

"Exactly. The poor chap. Sometimes he gets two of the same whatever the hell it is."

Hattie gave me a look that said she was concerned. I was fibbing a little bit of course. Most days my french fries were solid. I could sleuth with the best of them. But every once in a while the fries didn't fire right. Truth be told, everybody had an expiration date in the fight game. Some walked out with nothing more than a bruised ego. Some left with an unnatural gait and lazy eye. Some left in a body bag, with a hematoma, or suffering from some other malady that had dealt them one final blow in the squared circle. So I knew my days were numbered, and my quality of life was on the decline with each passing day. Maybe I had one more fight in me, or maybe it was twenty fights. No matter what, I'd be gone, and the show would go on.

If I had to choose my ending? I'd put my opponent in a body bag, then I'd go out in my own body bag, croaking from all the excitement. That'd add some sizzle to the pay-per-view.

"The struggle is real," Hattie said.

"Apples and oranges," I said.

"A couple more good shots and there'll be no more fruits to pick."

"I like that visual. Fruits are healthy."

Hattie typed something on her computer and then

retrieved something from her printer. "Water?" she said, pulling out another bottle.

"I'm fully hydrated," I said.

"Awesome." She sat back down. "Level with me here. What did you want to ask my boss?"

"A magician never reveals his secrets."

"It takes two to tango, champ."

Hattie was right, but at the same time I didn't trust her yet. Beware smoking hot chicks in auto bays. When the time was right perhaps I'd wax poetic and spill. She wasn't an amateur sleuth after all. She'd have to earn it.

"In poco tiempo," I said. "Macho have any vices?"

"What man doesn't?"

"Any fucked-up ones?"

"If you count drug use and banging other people's wives, then I'd say so."

"Maybe he's on a bender," I said.

"Could be, but that's his business. I know my duties here, and I gotta hold down the ship till he gets back. Furthermore, I have to protect the bays from carless peeps like you, throwing the crew off rhythm."

"The struggle is real," I said.

She rolled her eyes. "But his ass better come in later for payday. I still haven't set up my direct deposit, and I need a new phone."

"What kind of fruit?" I asked.

She was genuinely confused for a minute, then it dawned on her.

"Apple, man," she said. "You're something else."

"That's what she said."

Hattie tried to shoo me away, but I asked her about mobile deposits and she graciously gave me the scoop. I was amazed at how far technology had come, regardless of the fruit.

Then I switched gears.

"Where's Macho's place at?"

"Stalker."

"For real."

"Some mansion that only one of the workers has been to. Gates around the whole damned place and they never even let him in."

"When?"

"A few weeks ago. For some birthday party. The worker went home and bitched about it on the floor. Got cheated out of some luxury I guess."

Before I could ask more questions, somebody shouted, "Tranny leak!" Hattie got up from her chair and walked to the entryway. She stopped and looked back at me.

"Hey, I'm doing a late lunch after I deal with these assholes. You've made my day. You up for some grub?"

I accepted the invitation, and Henri and I left the office. On our way out of the bay, I sensed somebody watching me. A lifetime in the ring and a lifetime on the inside does that to you.

I looked over my shoulder, and I was right.

An S-class Mercedes with black tints peeled out of the parking lot.

5

Twenty minutes later I stood in line with Henri. The beauty of governmental agencies is that they create the appearance of efficiency and customer service. This, in turn, gives confidence to those taking time out of their day to address the banalities of vehicle registration, emissions testing, boat titling, and more. But the illusion wears off faster than Usain Bolt in his prime. Everybody must take a ticket, and when the ticket machine so happens to be out of tickets or no longer produces legible tickets, lunch time begins for the powers that be.

Translation: Anybody waiting in line is shit out of luck and better hope there's a seamless changing of the guard at the front desk, otherwise ghost chairs are real.

Henri knew all this already, so he entertained the line peeps while I continued analyzing my surroundings. My mind grabbed on to random minutiae at random times, and I wouldn't trade it for anything in the world. Except a lifetime supply of pancakes, but that wasn't in the cards right now.

The New Mexico Motor Vehicle Division colloquially

went by "MVD." It was a one-stop shop for all your road-riding needs and just like its Illinois counterpart that I knew as the "DMV," if you had the connects, you had the connects. Procedures were about as consistent as the Bears' quarterback play on Sundays.

But the beauty of being semi-famous is that not only do you know somebody, if you don't, you know somebody who knows somebody. Your team has their own team. So it was at times like this that I appreciated having Sims on payroll. I had a connect at the MVD who'd get me what I wanted. Still, first I'd have to wait in line and play the confused citizen in need of a driver's test. I had no problem showcasing my acting skills. But then I'd say the magic words, and *voila*, I'd school the system and get what I wanted.

The asshole who'd been stalking me outside Macho's shop.

It didn't take a rocket scientist to put it all together. See stalker, find stalker, get answers. Muy simple. A Mercedes S-Class right outside the shop burning rubber at the sight of me? I wasn't exactly a sight for sore eyes, but when a celeb and his dog invade your town asking about a man named Macho, all hell breaks loose. Find the car, find Macho. I was sure of it.

Otherwise, why the screechfest, right? The S-Class had almost decimated its chassis getting the hell out after I'd spotted it. I didn't believe in coincidences. They were like assholes, and you can fill in the rest, hombre. I'd been asking questions about the tire don, and somebody didn't take too kindly to my amateur sleuthing. Of course, there's two sides to every coin. Maybe it was Hattie's ex, jealous that I had gained such rapport with such a mesmerizing gal.

The line was moving now. The changing of the guard was seamless. Four people in front waiting for their golden ticket. Henri was wagging his tail, drooling like a boss. If I'd had a ball

I'd have played fetch with him to pass the time. But one of the guards didn't take too kindly to my companion.

"No dogs here," the desk lady said. She flared her nostrils and seemed of the same unsound mind as the previous occupant of that desk.

"I don't see any conspicuous signage," I said.

"Not today. I'm covering for Myrtle. Don't make me get security," she said.

The desk lady looked over her shoulder to some dude who thought Sun Chips and Cheetos qualified as lunch. He made it all better by downing his meal of champions with a splash of Diet Coke.

I smiled. While the average hombre cowered in fear and ran from trouble, I embraced every fucking second of it. I loved the uncertainty of it all, I loved the way blood coursed through my veins, and I loved the way my heart pumped with each breath.

I could take the dude any day of the week, but that would have been too easy. If the security guard came over I'd give him a lecture on service animals and their utility in a society filled with handicaps. I'd talk about the origin of service animals in eighteenth-century Paris, where they helped lead the blind, before they slowly came to perform all sorts of tasks. I'd show him my papers, and I'd show him Henri's tags and designations.

Acting was sweet.

Hell, I might even tell him that I was the Professor, and that I'd learned all this shit straight from the joint with all that time on my hands. Time for shit I didn't do. I'd mess with his head so much he'd wish he'd extended his lunch with Fritos, too.

But it wasn't meant to be. The security dude didn't look up from his newspaper. The desk lady bristled.

"Sir, I'm serious."

Then the masses did all the work for me.

"That's the champ," one of them said. "He did time for some bogus shit and now they gotta pay him."

"He knocked Juko straight on his ass," another one of them said.

They took out their phones and did what fruit phone people do. I took it all in stride. While much of what they said was true, I wanted to dispute the payment part. Sims was still waiting on my check, and things got complicated in the court system when your old lawyer had played both a superstar and a serial killer on the side. Perhaps the stars would align prior to my demise and I'd get my green. Till then, I had zero confidence in the bureaucracy.

A few of the golden ticket holders asked for autographs, and I obliged. I was on a roll today. Before the fall, I carried a Sharpie on me at all times. It allowed me to fine-tune my penmanship and never disappoint my legion of fans. But since I'd gotten out, I'd taken a much more lackadaisical approach. Where the autographs came, so would the tools for the job. That was my motto. Besides, I needed to develop my scrawl with various scrivener's tools.

Like the MVD swag.

I hopped to the front of the line and grabbed a pen taped to a clipboard. I motioned the masses forward and signed like a machine. Smile. Ask for name. Insert name. Sign name. Pose for photo. Rinse and repeat. I knew this would get a rise out of the desk lady, but that's how I rolled. I signed for the four people in front and then for the nine in back. When it was all said and done, I got to skip the line, and the desk lady was so flabbergasted that she pushed me off to the next station with my ticket.

I sat in one of the red plastic chairs and waited like a good citizen. I didn't sign for anybody else. Henri must have known that our turn was coming up because he stood still like a statue, staring at the number counter on the wall. If it was a big ole bag of venison, that counter would be out for the count.

My number was called.

I approached the glass and found myself facing a man in green spectacles with a goatee that would have put Confucius to shame. We stared at each other for a while, then I asked for my guy. The green spectacles man had no idea what I was talking about, and I pretended I had no idea what he was talking about. This was all part of the game. Your guy never wanted to out himself for fear of losing his esteemed position. Your guy could have been the biggest crook on the payroll, but the appearance of legitimacy mattered more than every shyster task completed over the years. It wasn't cool to openly defy procedure in the hallowed MVD.

Play by the rules and the goodies shall come.

I tried again.

"Lacy, Lacy, where's all that crazy?"

The green spectacles man shook his head and left the station. He pushed open a side door and disappeared for a few minutes. I had all day to find what I was looking for, so I stood there and tapped my right heel to the beat of a Luke Bryan song I had stuck in my head from my second Uber ride of the day. I would have tapped my left heel too, but the side door opened and a buff black dude with a green polo shirt and clean-shaven skin stepped up to the station.

"Sir, how can I help you at the MVD today?"

Another stare-down.

"Lattimore, oh Lattimore, wherefore art thou Lattimore?"

The green polo dude furrowed his brows, then smiled. "Sims told me to expect your candy ass. Crazy-ass Gedrin, you haven't changed one bit. How's it been, homie?"

"About as swell as some sherbet on a hot summer's day."

"What kinda shit you into now?"

I gave Lattimore Lacy the scoop.

"Trouble keeps following your ass," he said.

"That's what she said."

Lacy laughed and typed away at his computer. "How's the family?" he said.

"He's a ninety-three-pound bundle of joy," I said, glancing over at Henri. He was expecting a treat, but I was expecting some info about the S-Class. He gave me those puppy eyes again, and I caved. Boy, he still had it.

Lacy printed something out and handed it to me. "When's your next fight?"

"Whenever Sims gets his ass off the beach and sends the papers. He's in Crete trying to pick up the language. You wanna seat at the next one, you got it."

"I like that. Gedrin, we straight."

We shook hands, and I was gone. When Henri and I got outside, I glanced down at the paper.

The paper read, "Queso Holdings."

I smiled.

I hadn't eaten a quesadilla in forever.

6

Henri hopped in the car first. He went to his favorite spot, which was right behind the driver's seat. He drooled on the window, did three circles, and found his nook.

My favorite spot was the seat opposite Henri's. It gave me ample distance from the monster, and it allowed me to have a bird's-eye view of the driver. Maybe this harkened back to my time on the inside, where I always sat with my back to all walls. Full visual on all subjects at all times. DTA. Don't Trust Anybody. Or maybe it was because I wanted to analyze my driver's speed and tell him to hurry the hell up or slow the hell down.

I looked out my window and smiled. The sun was still out and its warmth radiated off the leather upholstery. There were two camps when it came to summer car riding. Those who wanted the AC going full tilt, and those who wanted the windows down.

I was definitely a windows-down kind of hombre.

I told the driver to crack the windows a few inches, but I

was met with silence. I repeated myself, and got more of the same. Then I looked over at the driver, and things got real interesting. Normally, a sane, human driver with even a sliver of customer service would look back and confirm my drop-off destination. That driver would then make sure I was comfortable, and both windows would be cracked pronto. I might nod my head or give an alternate address to mess with his head a little bit, but all in all it'd be a seamless exchange of information. It was a service business, after all. The topics on the ride would cover sports, weather, political assassinations, or my fights. The chat would get real boring at times, and pick up at others. I would stay out of politics, but would dive full-tilt into sports. That's how I played it. I could have been one hell of a commentator if it wasn't for the dress code. No way in hell would I wear suits every day like some abogado.

Hard pass.

The driver would then give his two cents' worth, and the song and dance would continue for the duration of my ride. That's how it went in all the taxis and Ubers I'd ever been in. But there's a first time for everything. Because when I looked over at the driver now... there was no driver. I saw just a phone, or maybe it was one of those tablets all the fruit people used. The thing lit up like a Christmas tree and words flowed across the page like it was an Etch A Sketch. I would have hopped out right there, if it wasn't for the dude who popped up from the passenger seat.

"Good afternoon, Ubervillain" the man said.

"Top of the afternoon to ya, stalker," I said. "You testing the damned thing, or will the bot get me to my place of business?"

"You're in luck," the man said. "Your ride was chosen for one of our pilot programs. The self-driving mechanism is really sweet. The ride's on the house today. All we ask for is some honest feedback for future rides."

The man started fiddling with some gadgets on the dashboard.

I didn't know what was worse. Trusting my fate to some robot, or trusting it to the man behind the robot. I decided on neither. I looked over the gadgets, analyzing every nook and cranny. I wasn't an expert in automobile parts by any means, but I had a good sense if the parts were shitty quality or not. Then Henri and I could always book another ride and live to tell the story.

I tried to find a fatal flaw in the parts to give me the go-ahead to bail, but then I realized that I had told Hattie the spot and the time. One of the worst things a gentleman can do is show up late to lunch with a lady. Chivalry and respect went hand in hand, and a promise is a promise.

"Book it, hombre," I said.

The tester man nodded and pressed some buttons on the tablet, and the car took off. The man explained some of its features, but I was holding on for dear life. Henri, on the other hand, didn't seem bothered by the affair. Life was a grand party, and he was a bit player. That, and the chap could sleep through an avalanche when he'd met his Uber limit for the day.

The car sped up at times and slowed down at others. The handling was decent, but that didn't make my stomach any less queasy. The light turned yellow at one of the intersections, and I braced for impact with a car turning through the intersection.

But the non-driver stopped on a dime.

"Good play," I said.

"The apparatus senses how to maneuver based on the driving conditions," the man said. "It's all sensors and thermal features and the works. Ain't getting anything by this thing."

"Does it sense my concern?" I said.

The man laughed. "Hell, it senses when my wife is gonna put me in the doghouse for the night."

I switched it up on him. "When can I test a flying car?"

I wasn't being serious. I could hardly get through this ride, but I was at least a bit curious.

The tester man beamed. "Our models predict by 2040 we may have some traction. The market is skyrocketing. Trillions of dollars being pumped into the tech space."

I cracked some joke about fender benders and the tech space and all the fruits taking over the world, and the tester man scribbled something down in his notepad. Maybe I'd get a chocolate for my troubles.

We passed a slowpoke in the right lane and then another one in the fast lane before finding the right lane again and coasting along smoothly. I still had my hand on the handle on the ceiling, but my grip was getting less tight by the minute.

"What brings you to Los Alamos?" the tester man said.

"Quesadillas," I said.

"We have a lot of those out here."

"What are the hottest spots?" If an amateur sleuth wants the scoop, ask the damned locals.

The tester man thought about it for a few seconds, then smiled.

"Well, Tapas Georges is really solid. You can't go wrong with Burrito Haven either."

The names didn't float my boat.

"What's the fanciest place in town?" I said.

"For tacos?"

"For anything." I figured that the queso man could be hiding in non-Mexican waters. Near the place that was on file with the MVD. The address I'd received from Lacy was shit. We'd passed it on the ride over. It was an empty lot. Which meant that the queso man wanted to shield himself from prying eyes like mine. That was cool, because I never quit. Find the queso man and maybe Macho was right around the corner.

The tester man thought about it some more, then nodded.

"Roody's Cafe is awesome."

I clapped my hands real loud.

"What are you doing?" the tester man said.

"Telling the bot to re-route," I said.

He shook his head and went into detail about how stopping it mid-ride could mess with the metadata and trip algorithms. He used a bunch of scientific words that bored me, but I took it in stride. After a while I was tempted to have Henri fix the data, but I let it be.

The tester man typed away on the tablet, and then luckily the thing re-routed.

We talked about sports and current events, but no politics this time. I was glad. I didn't have an ounce of energy for that crooked fest, though a part of me wanted to perhaps float a run as a water commissioner someday. H_2O is the most important part of any meal, and the citizenry needs access to top-notch water.

Life is filled with opportunities.

Five minutes later we reached Roody's Cafe. I texted Hattie the new spot, and she told me she'd be there in a couple minutes.

"I love those things," the man said, pointing to my Jitterbug.

Finally a man that got me. I pulled out some cash to tip the apparatus, but the man waved me off.

"Thanks for participating today," he said. "Treat your lady right at Roody's. Get the chicken Vesuvio."

He gave me a fist bump, the apparatus beeped a couple times, and the doors unlocked.

Flying cars would be even sweeter.

7

Hattie had changed clothes. She'd tossed her uniform in favor of tight black jeans, a light pink Henley, and a pair of white sneakers. If she was a nine before we'd made plans for lunch, she was a solid ten now.

I had no objection.

Roody's was the perfect choice for our midday meal. The place easily held the title of biggest venue on the block. Outdoor seating started at the curb and stretched all the way down to the alleyway behind the place, and the hubbub of traffic was muffled by all the social accord. The latest hip-hop tunes played from speakers in the background, and the waiters danced to the beat each time they came to serve. The tablecloths didn't have a speck of dust on them and beverage refills were a given.

Hattie sat with her legs crossed and I sat with my chair tilted forty-five degrees so I could have easier access to Henri. He was going to town on a puppachino and I was thoroughly enjoying rubbing his whiskers in the process.

Hattie took a long sip of her Coca-Cola. "I was looking

forward to the drinks spot you picked first, but this place is pretty cool."

"I don't drink in season. It ruins my pores." I smiled. I was lying of course. I drank after every fight. Quite heavily in fact. If pancakes were my biggest obsession, pulp-free OJ was a close second. I'd down so much juice after a fight I'd be pissing fluorescent orange hues. Vitamin C was the real deal.

But a gentleman needs to shield his vices on first dates. For brownie points.

Hattie frowned. "I call bullshit."

"You're a natural," I said.

"That's what he said."

I laughed, and Hattie returned it. A waitress came and took our orders. Hattie went with a turkey club on white bread. She parted her hair to the side, thumbed through the menu some more, and asked the waitress some questions.

Then she pulled the trigger.

"And he'll have a Reuben, hold the sauerkraut."

I knew right then and there that Hattie was the real deal. A woman who knows your order is a keeper. Maybe she'd subliminally messaged my old trainer Sal to get the scoop or maybe that asshole Sims. The fastest way to a man's heart is through his stomach. That's what he probably said.

I smiled, but I wasn't going to let her get off that easy.

"I wanted the chicken Vesuvio," I said. "Tops on the menu."

Hattie snorted. "Disgusting. I read Yelp before I got here."

I nodded. Too many fruit phones out there.

I realized that the more things changed, the more things stayed the same. Ever since I'd gotten out, I was a nomad. Different city, but the same calling. Justice. Righting wrongs. Sticking my head where others said it didn't belong. That's the way I was wired, and I didn't back down from anybody. If there was a question that irked me, dammit I'd find the answer.

So the more I stared at Hattie now, the more the movies played in my head. Gedrin again on the sleuth. Another female in the fold. Compatibility and more. Vibing. The images rushed by at a gazillion frames per second and never went out of style. I had no idea what this latest adventure with Hattie would bring, but I knew that she'd be a part of my next movie. No matter where our paths ended up.

Being me was extraordinary.

She took a piece of tissue out of her purse, spit her gum into it, and tossed it in her water cup.

"You're a mixer," I said.

"What?" she said.

"Gum and H2O. No rule against it, missy."

"It numbs some of the cola. Too much sugar in that shit. There's barely any water in my cup anyway."

I looked both ways like I was about to share a secret.

"I'm a sticker," I said. "Right under the table. No extra supplies needed."

Hattie rolled her eyes, and I shifted gears to what I'd come here for.

"How big is Macho?" I said.

"He's a famous tire YouTuber who has done quite well for himself. He's a millionaire, man."

"How many accounts does he have?"

"That's privileged information." Hattie held my gaze for a few seconds.

"Says the lady who led me right into the belly of the beast. Macho's office looked like shit. Maybe he wouldn't take too kindly to strangers and their canines visiting."

I knew that wasn't her office back at the shop, and now she knew that I was a complete wild card. If I didn't get what I wanted, what was to stop this semi-famous boxer dude from saying he'd waltzed right into Macho's office without an appointment or a care in the world? I could cry wolf and somebody would listen, somewhere. I had the connects after all.

Hattie knew the score. Job security was muy bueno.

"You do have some mass of brain left," she said. "He's got about ninety-three clients. Each week he picks up a few, give or take. Everybody wants to do business with the tire man."

"Who's his oldest client?" I said.

"No idea."

I figured his long-time customers knew his whereabouts.

The food came, and for a moment Henri thought he was getting all of it. He stared at me like I had the plague, and pools of saliva hung off his mouth like elongated Brussel sprouts. I enjoyed the show, but I knew he deserved at least a little piece of Reuben. I tossed it to him.

"For his service skills," Hattie said.

"Hell yeah."

Hattie bit into a piece of her club with the toothpick still in it. She narrowly avoided a tooth displacement, but I appreciated the brazenness.

"Does Macho have a shop out here?" I said.

Hattie shook her head. "He's picky about his spots. It's gotta sing to him. That's what he said once. Not much singing out here. Other than this cafe, not much action out here at all. A bunch of empty lots and failed businesses, then parks and suburbia. That's why Paco has accounts all over New Mexico."

"Where's the majority of them?" Find the concentrated accounts, cross them off, then go for the low-hanging fruit. The outliers. Making plays from the fringes where nobody else could see. That was Macho's play. I had a hunch.

"Most of them are around the flagship. Little used car lots

and small-time dealers. The occasional Audi off the highway or Mercedes. But not too many of those."

My mind was stuck on Mercedes, but then Henri barked at a fly and I forgot about it.

"How many actual accounts out here?"

Hattie finished two quarters of her club and placed the toothpicks neatly next to the pickle that was provided with her meal.

"Don't think there's a specific account out here, but the big man would always brag about schooling some badminton champion in Los Alamos."

"Preach."

"The taquito man. Some restaurant big shot that always got the best of him. But one day the big man schooled his candy ass in front of a large crowd. Big bucks were on the line. At least, that's the way he tells it. You think Paco got to the top being a pussy?"

"Pussies are no fun," I said.

Hattie held my gaze again, a little longer this time. "Lies, champ. Lies, I tell ya."

"True that." I grinned.

Henri asked for another piece of Reuben, and I obliged. A car blared its horn outside, and then the speakers started blasting country tunes.

"I hate this," Hattie said.

"I love me some taquitos," I said.

"Are you asking me out again? I love Mexican."

"I'm in season," I said.

Hattie smiled, and I got the check.

8

We never got Mexican. They didn't serve any at the badminton club in Los Alamos, and that wasn't on my menu anyway. Finding the queso man was. Hattie was disappointed at first, calling me "carless deceiver" a few times, then she snapped out of it when she realized that physical activity was in the cards for our expanded hanging session.

She flashed her pearly whites and made a few calls to clear the rest of her day at the auto shop. Being Macho's second in command apparently didn't mean shit. When she was all done, she was ready for the challenge. Damn, she was so fine with that racket in her hand.

I had a racket in my hand too, but I wasn't as graceful. My skill lay in rendering people comatose. I was a natural in basketball and football, but sports like tennis required a wee bit more finesse, which eluded me like solid quarterback play at Soldier Field.

I'd never played badminton before, but it was even tougher than tennis. The birdie was smaller and the racket too. Power paled in comparison to the precision required to place the birdie properly.

Hattie did some stretches and then served. If anybody was pissed at our choice of rackets and attire, they never showed it. Beauty pays in a myriad of ways.

I crushed the birdie out of bounds on my first swing. I flexed my biceps and danced with the racket.

"You suck," Hattie said. "One point for me."

"I'm just getting warmed up."

I smiled, and Hattie served again. I had no idea how the score worked or whether we took turns serving, and that split-second uncertainty made me whiff the birdie.

Hattie laughed.

"Another point for me. Damn, stick to the ring, dude."

Hattie tossed me the birdie, and I ran it around in my hands for a moment. It was an oddly shaped creature. But 'twas the way of the game. I threw it straight up in the air and used every ounce of patience I had to not crush that damned thing. The birdie floated down just above my head and then I swung, floating the birdie over the net into the back right corner of the playing area.

Hattie was flummoxed because she let it go thinking it was gonna go for the fences, but it landed just inside the line.

"I win," I said.

"Lucky point, dude." Hattie pulled her hair back in a pony-tail and did some lunges. She was wearing fuchsia shorts from the pro shop and they were muy bueno. I, on the other hand, was wearing my usual summer gear. Tight jeans and a muscle tee. Extremely versatile and just damned dashing, all around.

But no wonder I was losing. While my ensemble was solid, it didn't make me all that flexible.

Hattie had the edge in that department.

I served up the birdie again, and she crushed it back to me.

I waited and took something off my forehand. Hattie hit a nice backhand. Then I hit a forehand again. Another backhand. It went like that eleven times before I lost it for good.

The taquito man was here.

I was sure of it.

He walked onto the courts with a mustache that would make porn stars proud and a nineties Rolex on his left wrist. His outfit was all white. Tennis shoes. Shorts. Shirt. Headband. His hair was neatly coiffed and he oozed new money. His shirt had a small logo on the left breast with two tacos crossed in an 'X' formation. Just above it were the words "Tacos Grandes."

Short, to the point. Clear branding.

The birdie hit me square in the head.

"I win," Hattie said.

"Me too." I looked over to the taquito man, and Hattie smiled.

"Should we ask for his autograph?" she said. "He's real famous." She stuck her tongue out and rolled her eyes.

"I'm gonna ask him a question," I said.

"Knock your socks off, Sherlock."

"Don't mind if I do."

I ran the scenarios in my head. This was an uppity badminton club, so I couldn't just beat the shit out of the guy to get answers. I also couldn't just wait all day to get the scoop. Henri was in the pet room, slobbering on the glass overlooking the courts. He was well taken care of, but I never liked leaving him that long.

I chose option three. Indirect interference. I walked across the court to the linoleum bench the taquito man was sitting on. I got within three feet, but no more. A security wannabe held his hand out like he was directing traffic at the Pink Purse.

I could have taken him easily, but I had to stay the course.

The taquito man looked up and smiled.

"Ah, a new player at my club," he said. He straightened out the edges of his mustache as he spoke.

I rolled up the sleeves on my t-shirt, exposing my rock-hard muscle.

"My game needed some new challenges," I said. "Let's roll."

The taquito man laughed and pulled two white wristbands out of a duffel bag. He put them on and started doing stretches.

"I only play newbies to seven," he said.

The security honcho backed up. Left hook to the liver. That would do it. But I let it be.

"That's very macho of you," I said. I let the word hang, and taquito man knew exactly what was up.

"Excuse me a moment." He whispered something to the honcho and started walking toward the locker room. The honcho stepped between us, cutting me off.

The taquito's man's playing partners got on the court like it was another day at the office. They started warming up, hitting the birdie back and forth to each other with light strokes. I would have asked for a few pointers, but the honcho was cramping my space.

"They don't pay you enough to get hurt," I said to him.

"Is that a threat?"

"It's a promise."

I clenched my fists and was ready to give in to my natural skills, but Hattie stepped in.

She put her hands on the honcho's shoulders. "Forgive my boyfriend. He gets a little jealous with all these high rollers. He hasn't beaten a single one yet, but he'll always try."

She flipped her hair back and flashed her pearly whites the way all hot chicks do. Effortlessly and on autopilot.

The honcho much appreciated the physical touch, and I rolled with it.

"She's a keeper," I said.

"Whatever. Don't do anything stupid. My boss shits gold bigger than you."

"He must have hemorrhoids," I said.

"Whatever," he said.

He went back to the linoleum bench, took his phone out, and started playing with it.

Hattie wanted to play another game, but I wanted taquito man.

I went to the locker room.

9

The rich get richer. If the court was high-class, the locker room made it look like chump change. Three-thousand square feet of tiled marble floors, with walk-in mahogany lockers fit for a king. There were seven separate corridors of lockers and benches, followed by a row of showers in back.

I didn't get a chance to examine the first row of benches because a naked fat dude bumped into me.

"Pardon me," he said.

I wiped the condensation off of my shirt and trudged on. The next couple corridors were empty. The fourth consisted of two men about nine feet apart, taking their shower shoes off. The fifth had a cleaning person scrubbing tile so fast I thought he'd get a pinched nerve. The sixth was empty, and the seventh had a pushover dad talking shit to his kid about not hitting the birdie the right way. I wanted to give my two cents' worth, but I let it be.

The taquito man was long gone. He'd used his rich boy ways to sneak out some back door probably. I walked back along the corridors looking for all points of egress. I was tempted to ask the cleaning person, but he was even more determined than the greenskeeper with the turtle's nest.

The locker room started clearing out, and I walked over to one of the sinks and washed my hands. I wasn't one of those overly hygienic peeps, but the rackets didn't look too straight, so I figured soap would do the trick. I sang "Happy Birthday" in my head, and when I was finished, I stopped rubbing my hands and turned my attention to the mirror.

My face was developing some red splotches from where I'd ditched the sunscreen on the course this morning. Smooth skin is a privilege, and I'd thrown it away with my antics. Oh well.

I tossed some water on my face, and that's when I saw it. In the right-hand corner of the mirror, poking out slightly.

A sliver of Taquito man's white headband. Luck is part and parcel of the amateur sleuth game. There was no mistaking it. He was hiding in one of the lockers.

I dried my hands and waited for the pushover dad to clear out with his kid. They did, and that left me and the taquito man.

I walked over to the locker and sat on the bench in front of it. A respectable gentleman would come out and engage in conversation. He'd give his opinion on things, and I'd give mine. It'd go like that till things took a different turn. Maybe the respectable gentleman would resort to cheap tactics to get his way, or maybe he'd hightail it out of Dodge. In a perfect world, disagreements would be settled simply and efficiently. Discussions wouldn't beat around the bush.

But there was no movement from the taquito man.

I could hear him breathing heavily on the other side of the mahogany locker. Damn, I was that good. I hadn't even touched the hombre, and I had that effect. I basked in my game for another minute, then I got bored. I had shit to do and places to be.

I knocked on the locker.

Nada.

I knocked again.

Nada.

Then, instead of knocking a third time, I pulled the door open from the horizontal vents on top. The slats were the perfect size for my hands.

The taquito man flew out faster than a cheetah on the prowl. He stubbed his knee on the bench and winced in pain.

I stood there like an oak tree and didn't move a muscle.

He massaged his knee and his scalp, then slowly rose to greet me properly.

Without his security honcho he was just another rich bitch, and he knew it.

"Pleasure to meet the brains of the operation behind Tacos Grandes," I said.

"I'm sure."

"You always play mind games on these courts? I was ready for a challenge, and you pissed your pants, bro."

The taquito man wanted to say something, but nothing came out. He stood there in his all-white garb looking like a schoolboy in headlights.

But I wasn't gonna let him get off that easy.

I pinned him up against the locker with the palm of my hand.

"Where's your boy, Macho?" I said.

The taquito man tried to wiggle away, but I pinned him against the locker some more. He squirmed, but all those years taking money on the courts did absolute shit for his strength.

I let him off the locker for a moment, then I held up the Seiko.

"You both like vintage shit, huh?"

He didn't show any emotion at the sight of the watch, so I whacked him in the face with it.

"What the fuck, man?" He held his head, and I could see a solid welt forming above his right eyebrow.

"Where's your boy?" I repeated. "I don't like repeating myself."

"I haven't seen him in forever," he said.

He sat down on the bench.

"Cut the shit," I said. "You pack this court with your rich-ass friends, and then when Macho came in you found your patsy."

"Not at all," he said.

"How many times did he show you up before you decided to make an example out of him? Can't ruin your cred."

"Fuck you," the taquito man said.

I swatted his ear like he was a pesky fly on a hot summer's day. He fell off the bench and clutched his ear and his head this time.

"One more wrong answer and I get Henri."

"Who the hell is Henri?"

"A magician never reveals his secrets."

I clenched my fists, and the taquito man covered up instinctively. Then he caved.

"He's been MIA lately. Matters of the heart," he said.

"Do tell," I said.

He opened his locker back up and pulled out an ice pack. I let him use it.

"We used to play here a few days a week. The after-seven crowd was fierce. But that's not what he came here for."

For a second I wanted to make a sports analogy, then I understood.

"You wanted to eat Macho's ass and when he wouldn't let you, you made him disappear?"

The taquito man's face was redder than pomegranate now. He looked around the locker room as if the walls could hear his confession.

"Who are you?" he asked.

"A man with a question."

"No, seriously."

"A man with a question who happens to love pancakes and trouble."

The taquito man shook his head like he was up against a force too strong. Then he nodded a couple times to himself before speaking.

"Paco didn't want me. There's a lot of gays here who are big-time. I'm a small fish at the end of the day. He wanted somebody else. You find that dude and you'll get the answer to your question, pancake man. You look so sexy when you're mad by the way. I can tell you ooze pussy all day, but if you ever come around, there's always a place for you at this club."

"In your dreams, hombre. But I appreciate the compliment." I'd never swing to the other side of the fence, but I had zero objections to those who did. To each their own.

"What's his name?" I said.

"Hell if I know. My bet's on the copper though. He'd play Thursdays and Fridays and lose every fucking time. The asshole would flash his gun and badge before he hit the showers. Lot of curious folk out there. He wouldn't shut up either. Bragged about some isolated piece of real estate on the Quemazon Trail. Exclusive, I guess. Paco loved that shit. Wherever there's wealth and power you can bet your ass he's there. He runs in bigger and bigger circles."

"And you never got a chance to profess your love."

"When I saw him in the parking lot one time waving the copper's shotgun, that was the end of my quest."

"Good call. How much are your quesadillas?" I asked.

"What?"

"At Tacos Grandes. I might pick up some comida before I head to Old Faithful."

"You're really something. The place is closed right now for in-person dining. Long lunch breaks to hit that birdie will do that."

He told me how much the quesadillas were, and then he explained to me how to order them from the app. I showed him the Jitterbug, and after a bit of frustration he set me up with an account to order any time.

"I hope you find him," the taquito man said. "Aside from him being a showboat, he was a pretty cool guy. Worked his way up from the fishing docks way before he got into tires. Gotta respect the dudes that work their asses off and make it from nothing. Not easy to get in this big boy club. If I was in the tire game, I'd have worked with him. He knows his shit."

I nodded, and the taquito man shook my hand. He said some platitudes that I forgot in a few seconds, and then he went back out to the court, sans ice pack.

10

The Quemazon Trail was a hidden gem amongst a plethora of gems in this world. Lightly trafficked and roughly six miles long, it was the perfect place for the beginner hiker to improve his or her game.

I wasn't a hiker by any means, but the more people I saw gutting it out, the more confident I became. I walked along the trail taking in the tall embers and the thickets and the lake, and I was at peace.

I'd left Henri and Hattie behind at the club. The former wanted more play time, and the latter challenged the taquito man to a marquee matchup in front of all his groupies. With each step now I heard the birds chirping and the branches breaking off in the distance. Wildlife was really something.

I knew Macho's lover was up in these parts, so the journey made it all the more rewarding. When I found him, I'd tell him just how close I'd come to missing my speech at Dobermans for Life. Then I'd show him the watch and get the answers I wanted. Hell, I might not even need to go far. Maybe Macho was hiding in the master bedroom.

As I trekked along, I worried about the answers I'd get. A part of me said the Seiko was nothing more than a replica amongst an avalanche of replicas. But another part of me said that there was more meaning behind it all.

There was a connection to my dad. I felt it in my bones somehow, like a prescient wizard with his eyes over the crystal ball. I wanted to know every detail. It was in my nature. But the more I thought about it, the more I wanted to hold back.

Fact: Every person has demons. Could I handle the truth and nothing but the truth? Could I handle the possibility that Papa Gedrin was anything but a legend on the high seas? I pressed on up the gravel path, passing four bikers, two long-distance runners, and one rollerblader. I wanted to race the rollerblader, but I let it be. The hombre had the blades with the stoppers on them, so it'd be too easy.

The trail got narrower as I approached the tail end. One of the beauties of the place was that as the six-mile trek petered out, the foot traffic followed suit. Gone was my motivation to gain time on my fellow hikers, but now the feeling was replaced with something far better.

Just me and good ole Mother Nature.

I stared at the clearing around me and smiled. I'd come a long way from Pontiac. I used to wince at the sound of a carburetor or a graham cracker breaking. That's how fucked-up it is on the inside. But with each passing minute, I'd regained my confidence. I'd built my champion body back up, one brick at a time. From the Zemun to the cutman, I'd weathered it all. That's how I rolled.

A wise man once said that time is the greatest counselor of all. I wholeheartedly agreed.

I trudged on, the trail narrowing further. The taquito man had said that Macho's lover boasted about the prime real estate out on the trail. In the real estate milieu, secluded location and scenic view equals unparalleled real estate. Which equals a fancy price tag and an even fancier sense of entitlement. Macho's lover's palace was tucked away somewhere in these woods.

I started jogging to switch up the routine. Badminton wasn't exactly the most taxing of sports, and I loved the excitement. I jogged for three minutes, then went back into a walk. Then a jog, and another walk. My head was throbbing a little from Roody's cuisine, but I kept at it. I repeated the cycle a few times, and when I got to the end of the trail, everything changed.

I spotted a cabin two hundred feet away up in the foothills. The only way to get there was to take a tiny dirt path that looked like it had been trudged out by the lone resident who staked his claim there. A rope cordoned off the path from the rest of the foothills to keep all enemies out.

Which was great for me because I was a neutral observer. Amateur sleuths in need of information must play their cards the right way, hombre. I looked around. Nobody in sight. It didn't take me long to make my decision.

I hopped the rope and followed the path. A dog howled in the distance, penetrating my soul and making Henri sound like a pre-pubescent boy by comparison. The dirt trail wound in circles toward its destination. I continued on.

The dog howled again.

And again.

I got closer and closer.

Cabin man had a big-ass canine, that was certain. I wanted to ask what the man was feeding him.

But I didn't get the chance.

Somebody clubbed me in the back of the head and I crumpled like a couple of broccoli sticks.

A lifetime in the ring had taught me to expect the unexpected. People bum-rushing the ring. People using padded gloves. Big-ass counterpunchers. To put it plainly, a fighter can give superhuman amounts of punishment, but a truly special fighter can *take* superhuman amounts of punishment and keep coming back for more.

I was one of them.

I sprang back to my feet and saw the man who'd hit me. He was in his early sixties, with cowboy boots, boot-cut jeans, and a neatly coiffed goatee. He was like Chuck Norris incarnate. I figured he was cabin man.

"What the fuck you doing on my property, son?" he said with a snarl, flaring his nostrils like a rhinoceros.

I wasn't fazed. "Going for a dip, cabin man. Do you mind?"

That was all he needed to hear. He reached behind him into some bushes and pulled out a shotgun. He cocked it the way gun peeps do, then he pointed it right at my face.

"Give me one good reason I shouldn't blow your brains out."

"I don't have much brain left," I said. "Less than double digits."

I explained a little bit of my boxing history. The man wasn't enthused. Then the dog appeared, and I was right on the money. He was a big-ass dog. A Belgian Malinois to be exact.

The Belgian leapt through the air and I ducked and rolled at the exact moment, causing the canine to hit the man's shotgun.

Cabin man then charged me, but I got him with an uppercut. He staggered back and charged again. I got him with another uppercut. The man was too slow and too fucking old. But one thing was certain.

This was a lawman, and a lawman never quits. At least the old-school ones don't.

The lawman bear-hugged me, and we both slipped off a

piece of rock and tumbled into a thicket. I thought I had the upper hand, elbowing and thrashing away at my quarry.

It was all a mirage.

You see, a man might bring the fight to another man, but if that same man doesn't know the territory, it's a fool's errand. When we landed somewhere at the bottom of the thicket, the man pulled a knife out of a hole in the ground and pressed it to my throat.

"Who the fuck sent you? Speak or I slit your fucking throat."

I thought about the perfect line, but I decided against it given the circumstances.

The truth shall set you free.

"Queso Holdings," I said.

11

The cabin didn't have a coffeemaker, microwave, or dishwasher. But the roughly seven-hundred-square-foot abode was decorated top to bottom. The ceilings looked like they were straight out of the Stone Age with their Neolithic figures, and the walls were covered with a plethora of taxidermy displays that hung like badges of honor, radiating testosterone and bravado. On the left side of the cabin were the smaller players in the animal kingdom: squirrels, rabbits, and snakes. On the right side stood the big boys: foxes, deer, and bears.

"Been a long time since I've had a visitor," the man said.

He walked over to the kitchen and opened up one of the cabinets. He fished in there for a few seconds before pulling out two glasses. He eyed them for prints, then ran the sink.

I stood by a wooden fireplace, my eyes still fixated on the bears. Chills ran down my spine. The man either had serious game with his shotgun, or he was friends with hombres who did.

The man came back and handed me a glass.

I don't do tap water, but sometimes an amateur sleuth has to bend the rules. I smiled and took a sip.

"The ambience here must bring many a passerby," I said. "Looky-loos and nature types."

The man snorted.

"No sirree. Not on my property. Those runners can be damned. Only reason I let you slide was you could take a lickin', boy. Never in all my years have I seen someone take a dive like that. That commands respect and a proper introduction."

He held his hand out.

"Yoko Fester," he said.

I nodded and told him my name.

He didn't recognize it.

"The world is an extraordinary place," he said.

I nodded.

Then the Belgian Malinois came into the cabin and sniffed me up and down like I had the plague. I did what I did best in these situations. When a stranger's canine approaches, I stand still as a statue. This allows the canine to fulfill his curiosity, and allows me to keep my limbs intact. I'd gotten too cozy with a stray Rottweiler during my youth, and I'd paid the price.

The Belgian sniffed to his heart's content, then licked my palm. I was in the club.

"What do you feed this monster?" I said.

"Doggo likes rabbits," Fester said. "I've tried to expand his palate to deer, but he refuses."

"What about snakes?" I said.

Doggo gave us both a look, then ran back outside.

"He spits them out after one bite," Fester said. "It's an acquired taste, boy."

Fester sat down in the recliner next to the fireplace and propped his feet up. I would have followed suit, but there wasn't another recliner or couch in sight. I stood there, squeezing the life out of my glass of water, while Fester chilled like a boss.

"Now," he said, "before I give you a taste of some of my stew—it's been on the stove for quite some time and I would hate for it not to be appreciated by a visitor—let's get down to brass tacks. What brings you by, boy? And don't give me that queso meso shit again. I could sniff that shit out in a heartbeat back before these here knees started singing. I didn't play, and I certainly didn't let anybody get by easy."

"Fed or statie?" I said.

I didn't play either.

Fester eyed me for a few seconds, like he was buying time to see if I passed the test. I furrowed my brows in response, and then Fester bit.

"Thirty-two years. Statie," he said. "I patrolled them highways in this great state. Third watch. Lot of nutjobs out there, but the man upstairs must've liked me. I never saw any action. Closest I came to fireworks was giving Liquor Control Act violations to all the fine local establishments playing it crooked around Los Alamos. Them suits always knew what to say and how to say it."

I cut to the chase.

"Did Macho fuck your pension?"

This shifted the conversation quickly and jarred Fester for a moment. But that was my intention. I came here to find out where in the blue hell Macho was, and what connection did Fester have with him.

Fester put his glass down on a dilapidated coffee table, and for a moment I thought he'd reach behind the recliner and go all shotgun on me again.

But he just rocked farther back in his seat and smiled.

"Ah, there's the rub," he said. "A lawman never escapes his

past. No matter how much good he does, there's always somebody in the way who wants to bring it all crashing down."

"Macho had a lot of enemies," I said.

"When you run the town, it's hard not to."

"When's the last time you saw him?"

"Three weeks ago, boy. Good riddance."

Fester gave me the full scoop. They'd gone their separate
ways, and it was mutual.

"The man only cares about his damned self," Fester said.
"All about his fucking name and those tires. But I know the
real Paco. The one who'd go to the strip clubs every
Thursday and pay the bouncers to give him some action.
Him and the pussy never mixed. He had some side piece, but
he could barely get it up. By design. He was swimming in
dick."

"And some dick did him in?" I asked.

"You bite off more than you can chew, you're bound to get
fucked the wrong way. Yessirree. But boy, don't go chasing
ghosts you can't catch. That man has a lot of clout in this town,
and he can damned near make sure you lose your pension on
top of it. I barely got out alive."

"His YouTube videos suck."

"Ain't that the truth. Society is a strange animal. One man's
shit is another man's treasure. I'm serious, boy. Leave the detec-
tive work to the professionals."

I'd heard that one before.

Fester got up from the recliner and walked over to the fireplace. He pulled an eight-by-ten photo from the wall. It had a
mauve frame and it hadn't been dusted in ages. Which was
perfect, because with a guest in tow Fester used the opportunity to wipe the frame down with the bottom of his shirt.

I took a closer look now at the picture, and there was Fester,
in his statie uniform, all smiles. With him was Doggo, tongue

out like a boss. And Macho was right in the middle, flaunting a fanny pack and a gold chain around his neck.

"Two months dating, at this point," he said. "We went over to Chizotlan Lake, ran a boat, had some brewskis, and did some water skiing. Never thought I'd try the damned thing, but that man was always a good persuader and he loved the water. Brought him back to his time on the docks. But when you're with someone long enough you see their true colors. Then you either stay the course or you want out. Paco knew what I was, but he never accepted what *he* was. He'd kiss me when nobody was looking and he told me he loved me when nobody was around. Secrets were his damned thing."

Fester pointed to the northern stern in the picture.

"We made plans to go to Europe. He loved pasta and wanted to take an authentic class straight from the experts. We booked everything. First class with all the leg room. And fucking beds too. Then the day of the flight, the asshole no-shows. I call him up and he ends it right there. Over the phone. He wasn't gay, he told me. He couldn't live that life. Boy, the man is bad news. He swore he'd fuck me if I outed him to the world. So I quit the force and fixed up this here cabin. I thought I was clean as a whistle again, but he still fucked with my pension date."

"Revenge is a dish best served ice-cold," I said.

"I like you, boy."

Fester took another sip of his water. I followed suit, then I took the Seiko out of my pocket. I showed it to him and told him about my dad.

Fester eyed it for a long time, the way a jeweler does before denying the piece's authenticity.

Then he shook his head.

"The man loved his watches, but he'd recycle them like candy. Every week, new bling on his wrist. One week a high-end, the next week a pawn-shop item. Boy, millions of people have those initials. Rocco Siffredi, for one. Top entertainer in the world. Adored around the world for his flexibility. I bet the asshole cheated on me for that famous ass."

It was a sound theory, but the more theories in your head, the more you stray from what your gut is telling you.

Macho was sending me a message.

12

The Quemazon Trail was quiet on the way back. It was like Mother Nature knew of my dealings with Fester and wanted me all alone in my thoughts. I didn't exactly have a royal flush, but I'd gotten little snippets about Macho. A snippet followed by a snippet followed by another snippet could lead to something.

One thing was clear. Macho was a con artist. He played both sides of the fence and tried to play goody two shoes afterward. He'd tossed Fester aside like a box of leftovers, but not before he'd gotten what he wanted from him. Men like Macho were the shittiest humans because they were all ego all the time. Emotions be damned.

Maybe he did cheat with Rocco Siffredi.

I walked ten more steps and then I heard life again. Twigs were crackling, the birds were back in song, and in the distance I could hear the thump-thump of a solid pair of running shoes on the gravel. The walk back to where I'd come from was a few more minutes. Then I'd Uber it the hell out of Dodge.

I'd go back to the playroom and tip the workers extra for

taking care of Henri. I'd share some platitudes with Hattie and figure out my next move. Maybe I'd invite her to watch my speech tonight. Every woman loved a man in a suit proselytizing to the masses. Charisma and charm. Or maybe we'd do Mexican the right way. Quesadillas and enchiladas and all the trimmings. Taquito man would need the pick-me-up after Hattie schooled his ass on the court.

But an old dude once said the best-laid plans of mice and men often go awry. Life gives you melons sometimes. That's another fucking saying on par with the first.

My picturesque walk on the Quemazon Trail came to an end. I stopped in my tracks when I saw it.

A dead animal.

Roadkill, but with no actual cars on this trail, I guess it better qualified as hombre kill. I walked up to the carcass and examined it from all angles. A lifetime in the ring and on the inside made me immune to the sight of blood. Death, too. The clock hit zero sometimes, and everybody had an expiration date.

The wound looked fresh. Right in the heart. An arrow right to the sweet spot. This poor animal's death had been no more than an hour ago. Some asshole who probably thought he was a big man. I leaned closer, and for a moment I thought about pulling out the arrow. I thought of Henri. If an arrow ever pierced his skin, I'd pull it out faster than you could say hola.

But there was no hope here. The deed was done, and any effort on my part to minimize suffering had long since passed. I looked around the trail for any passersby.

Nada.

I heard the birds again and the leaves.

And that's when everything changed.

A lawman not named Fester came out of the thicket. He wore a beige cowboy hat over a neatly pressed dress shirt with a breast pocket. He'd topped off the ensemble with some wrinkly denim. From the looks of it, he was more toward the rookie end of the spectrum, but I had to give him props for the fashion. Fashion is hard to come by in the middle of nowhere.

"I've been looking for ya," the lawman said.

He cracked a smile, and I didn't return it.

"I want a lawyer," I said.

I'd learned the magic words long ago. Say them and you stood a chance at making it out alive. Of course, it hadn't always worked out that well for me over the years, but the more you invoked the power of the suit, the better. A chance is a chance.

The lawman laughed.

"Only the guilty need lawyers," he said.

He walked fully out of the thicket and onto the trail. I sized him up. I could take him in a heartbeat, but there was the whole legal impediment. While I never batted an eye when it came to introducing myself properly to the citizenry during times of strife, I drew the line with the blue. They could concoct so many charges the statute book would complain.

I wouldn't resist or obstruct, but I sure as hell was gonna make him work for it.

"Never break bread with a badge," I said.

The lawman seemed to accept the point, then walked over to the carcass. He looked down at it, shaking his head.

"The javelina is an endangered species," he said. "Very few left out in these here parts. So few in fact, that hunting season is restricted. Big game, short window out here, you see? Forty-five days and that's all she wrote. You get caught with a javelina out of season, boy do things take a turn for the worse."

He spat at his boots.

"The javelina is an exquisite creature," I said. "Too exquisite to meet its maker so early in life."

The lawman didn't understand my creative diction, but he

didn't give a shit. I saw "New Mexico Game and Fish" written near his breast pocket. Ah, the wannabe protector of the species.

He'd picked a sunny day to stake his claim at least.

"What we have here is a dilemma of epic proportions," he said. "I have two wits say you shot this here javelina and dumped the bow. That's very compelling. A stranger on this trail. A big, funny-looking one too. How much your mama feed you, boy? We have honest folk in these here parts. When the honest folk speak, I reckon it's time to listen."

He smiled like he was the smartest man on this trail.

I wasn't letting him get off that easy.

"Where are these law-abiding citizens to ID me?" I said. "Bring them here for a show-up. Have them point to me as the javelina man." I raised my hands up and curled my palms for effect.

The game protector got schooled for a second, but he recovered.

"Probable cause is a pissy standard. Luckily for me, there's a way to get around all these semantics. See, I merely need reasonable suspicion you're committing a crime to detain you for further investigation. That's a lower standard, if you're keeping track, stranger. Let's go through it, just to make sure you get it. You by the javelina. Arrow in the javelina. Two wits saying you killed the javelina. Hell, it's a slam dunk."

"How many bald eagles you save today, hombre?"

That did it. He cuffed me and put them on extra tight just because. I'd been through the wringer before, but never in New Mexico. Let the fun begin.

I had more than a hunch that whoever had planted the arrow in the javelina's heart had planted the game protector too. An arrival at the exact moment I stopped in my tracks?

Hell no.

The protector led me through the rest of the trail. He said some stupid things to me that I don't remember and I said some hilarious things to him that he probably doesn't remember. The walk to the end of the trail took three minutes. The scenery was ruined.

Not a single hiker, runner, or animal greeted us. I wanted Fester to fly out of the clearing and put a stop to this shit, but that moment never came. Instead, the wannabe Fester put me in the back of a cop car. One of those old-school, super-wide ones with the makeshift light on top.

I didn't have time to analyze the upholstery.

When I looked out my window, I saw the same Mercedes from the auto shop.

13

I was placed in a holding cell that smelled like two decades of refrigerated piss. I knew the score. This wasn't my first rodeo. Enter any correctional institution and the plethora of aromas will threaten one's sanity and sinuses. The sooner a new resident of the bars accepts the facts, the sooner said resident can get back to surviving the whole thing.

I was chill, running the images of the Mercedes in my head again. Coincidences definitely were like assholes. The messenger couldn't have been more clear. Fuck with us and this is what happens. A trip to the Ritz.

I smiled. I enjoyed messages mucho and couldn't wait to keep on the sleuth. Every setback was yet another page for my scrapbook.

I stood a foot from the bars now, staring out at the badges typing on their computers. They crinkled their noses and tapped so hard on those keys, the whole building should have complained. Every so often they took breaks to text on their phones and chat with their desk mates.

The desks were a putrid display of architecture—what did you expect on a government salary—and sat diagonal to each other. Two badges per quadrant, and four quadrants total spaced across the cells. After a few minutes the count dwindled down to four badges, and a few minutes after that it dwindled down to just two.

I was biding my time, waiting for my spot. I knew precisely when to go for it. Ho-hum-tickety-hum. I gripped my hands tightly on the bars. And three minutes later it was time. The room had just one badge left. The truly dedicated one. He looked more genuine than the game boy on the trail, but stranger things could happen out in New Mexico.

I knew exactly what I was going to say and when I was going to say it. But first, let there be the opposite of melons. Let there be riches.

"You're blocking the sun, asshole," some drunken hillbilly said.

I didn't even turn. Common sense would say to turn and spot the threat and dispatch it accordingly. Always have your eyes on the lookout. Like a pack of hyenas circling its prey. Analyze, document, neutralize.

But I never used common sense, and I wasn't about to start now. I lived my life by pure instinct, and I'd managed to make it this far. I was a pancake aficionado champion and nobody was taking my throne. The hillbilly was the distraction I needed to set my plan into motion. Of course, there wasn't a window in front of me, but you can always count on a drunken hillbilly to be in lockup, at least for one night.

'Twas the way of the world.

I waited for the hillbilly to make another move. I could throw down with anyone, but it was in situations like these that I had to temper that reflex. At least for a few seconds. If the world didn't know by now, it was pow and lights out in seconds for the untrained fighter. It wasn't fair at all. But fair was the forbidden word in the fight game.

No crying in this game.

Just bring it.

I spotted the badge leaning back in his chair and stretching his back out. Hillbilly, oh hillbilly, wherefore art thou, hillbilly? If he came at me with weaponry of any kind, then things would get a tad bit hairier, but I'd still get the job done. I was the Professor, remember?

I waited and waited and waited and waited. It felt like an eternity behind those fucking bars, but that's all part of the ploy. No clocks down in lockup. No light. No hope. They wanted you to submit and be an orderly prisoner.

Yeah, right.

When I finally realized that the hillbilly was waiting for me to make the next move, I pounced on it. It takes two to tango.

I kicked the bars with the heel of my shoe.

Nada from the rookie.

I kicked them again, getting more toe than heel this time.

The rookie looked up.

"I want pancakes," I said. "Least your fine department could do after you fucking didn't read me my rights on that trail."

I heard murmurs of agreement behind me. In addition to the hillbilly, there were three other fine citizens who'd happened to get caught up in the mean ole criminal justice system. Perhaps they were guilty as all hell, but not in my book. They were innocent till proven guilty.

That's the way our system works, hombre. In theory, anyway.

And those innocents deserved some entertainment.

"Keep hitting the bars, you won't get your bologna," the

rookie said. He chuckled like a schoolboy and went back to his computer.

I smiled.

Just where I wanted him.

"Pancakes have been a staple of mine for quite some time, officer, but I'm thinking of making the switch to waffles soon. I hear there's some excellent waffle makers out on the market these days. Presto, and breakfast is served. I'll settle for a Belgian *waffle*."

I kicked the bars as hard as I could on the word "waffle," and while it didn't affect the rookie that much, it sure affected the hillbilly.

I knew it would.

He sprang up from his slumber and hobbled toward me. "I said you're blocking my sun, asshole. You can't be blocking my sun. Only so many sunny days in here, and you have to take advantage."

The hillbilly spit as he talked and his gums looked like licorice.

"You don't wanna Belgian waffle?" I said.

The hillbilly had had enough. He threw one of the laziest punches I'd ever seen. It floated in the air like a paper airplane and missed its destination badly. I'd expected nothing less.

Now, I could have gone easy on the hillbilly and explained to him all the nuances of Belgian waffles and why I had a dilemma, having been a pancake connoisseur my whole life. Switching wasn't an easy thing. My taste buds were quite deli-cate, and my stomach was too. Besides, gluten-free pancakes were in vogue, and I'd decided on the ride over to the station that I'd take Hattie out again and try the fluff that was all the new rage.

But a plan is a plan, and the poor hillbilly had to pay a price in that windowless cell.

After his punch missed, I gave him a shot in the right kidney. He buckled over like a sorry sack of potatoes. Then he got back up. The liquid courage was helping him, and I'd planned for this as well.

The hillbilly charged, and I pivoted off my left foot and pushed him right into the bars. The innocents were getting their money's worth.

The hillbilly wobbled for a few seconds before gaining some form of equilibrium. He stood tall, blood pouring from his nose. The rookie woke up, sprang from his desk, and pulled out the keys to the cell.

But I wasn't done yet.

There's still the big finish.

The hillbilly threw a hard right, and I slipped it and countered with a playful left hook. By my standards.

The hillbilly never got up.

The rookie pulled me out of the cell.

The innocents started chanting, "Waffles, waffles, waffles."

I flexed my biceps as more badges piled into the holding area. Words were exchanged and fingers were pointed. Paperwork was filled out and more computers were put to use.

Meanwhile I was placed in an empty cell right across the way. I was placed in solitary, and in this little land of who knows where, that meant a hilarious view of all the carnage I'd caused—and a carton of OJ.

I didn't get waffles, but hydration is a start. I leaned back on the bench and stretched my legs out. What a day. I sat there, pondering my next move to escape the place, when a badge walked right in front of me. It wasn't the game boy from the trail or the rookie from earlier.

The badge read "Warden."

"I've got a present for ya, champ," he said.

"Does it come with Belgian waffles?" I asked.

He unlocked my cell.

14

The warden handed me a dusty placard. It had the number three on the front with a big lanyard holding it together.

"Put it on that 'roid neck of yours," he said.

"I'm all natural, hombre."

"Why do all the out-of-towners cause so much trouble in my jail? First fight I've had in lockup since we re-did the place twenty-seven years ago." He cinched his belt, and it was still loose on him.

"I appreciate what you did with the place. Nobody's escaping anytime soon."

"Wise guy. After today who the hell knows. Word travels quick amongst your ilk."

He curled his bottom lip and flared his nostrils. I wasn't surprised. The innocents might have had the presumption in the court of law, but in the court of public opinion they were guilty as hell.

That included me.

"What's my bond?" I said.

"No bond for strangers in this here town."

He held my gaze and didn't back down.

"My lack of residency is an asset, not a detriment."

Truth. The fact that I had no official residency was the greatest boon of all. I packed light and visited all the fine states in the nation. Little by little I attacked my bucket list the way a pack of hyenas attacked its prey. New city. New motel. New memories. I didn't want it to stop. I had a million more places on my list.

First I had to get out of the game warden's grasp.

He tapped his knuckles against the cell.

"Up, wiseass."

"I have no residency," I said.

"We know. Up. Now."

He stepped into the cell and put his hands on his hips. The rookie didn't carry a gun on him—probably something about liability and lockups gone wrong—but the warden did. He ran the show, and if anything went wrong he'd be the one to fix it.

I could have continued being a hard-ass in the cell, but I obliged him. I was genuinely curious where this would all lead. Maybe he'd give me a ham sandwich or even that Belgian waffle if I played nice. Give the goods on some local dealer or some shit, and I'd be scot-free. I was great at spinning tales of fiction. Then again, maybe he'd toss me in a dungeon and Henri would never make it to Dobermans for Life. The poor chap would cling to Hattie faster than a junkie on speed.

"Sims can post my bail," I said. "You have the Jitterbug. Make the call and he's here in a heartbeat with all that cash. Little extra, too."

The warden had a scowl on his face.

"Where you're going, there ain't no bail."

He led me down the hall, past the innocents, who were

tapping the cells and raising their fists in unison. I fist-bumped one of them.

"Hands!" the warden shouted, smacking my hand down. He wasn't taking any chances this time.

I wanted to give him a left uppercut right there, but that would have been too easy.

He took me by the arm and led me down a long, desolate hallway that would have made Stephen King proud. Dusty lightbulbs flickered on and off and showcased the path like cathedral spires. The warden walked me past three empty interview rooms. Standard-grade railroad central. Metal tables with metal chairs bolted into the floor. A paint job from forty years ago. Dirt from all the travesties that had taken place in these rooms.

We stopped at the fourth interview room. The decor was similar to all the rest, except for the fact that the chairs had fresh red paint on them. A "Fresh Paint" sign gave me the clue. I had no idea which lucky chair I'd take, but I didn't have to wait long.

The warden had a conscience.

"One more, champ," he said. He dragged my arm and we walked farther down the hall. Ten steps later we stopped in front of a black iron door. The warden knocked, and I heard something unintelligible from the other side.

The door opened a tad.

A code of sorts was given.

Then the warden pushed me into complete darkness. I couldn't sense any movement around me and wondered why they were fucking me like this. I'd been through the wringer before, but never in pitch darkness.

There's a first time for everything.

"Walk three feet backward, turn left, and hold position," the warden said.

"Should I curtsy too?" I said.

"Walk the fuck back there."

I did as I was told. I closed my eyes and guesstimated three feet and took my steps. I nailed it perfectly, then turned to my left and waited. While the average human was uncomfortable with long periods of silence, I relished every moment of inactivity and solitude. The uncertainty brought out the rush, and the rush was muy bueno.

As I waited, my mind went to Hattie again, and Henri and Macho and the Seiko. My synapses flashed faster than a cheetah on the prowl, and I wondered how sharp my mind could have really been if it wasn't for beating brains for a living and getting beat in return. Life was a grand parade.

The lights snapped on, blinding me for a second. I was surrounded by seven men. They weren't exactly the innocents from the holding cell, but they were damned close. They were other accused gentlemen, and they all wore placards around their necks with different numbers on the front. The men were instructed to stand a couple feet apart from each other and face the warden.

Hell, I was in a damned lineup.

The warden came out of the shadows and smiled.

"Gentlemen, it will be just a moment as a special somebody comes to the booth. Stand the fuck straight and eyes on the glass." He nodded toward the Plexiglas in front of us. It was the classic see-through glass, at least on the opposite side. On our side, we couldn't see shit. But that was by design in the great state of New Mexico and everywhere else in the USA.

I looked around at the men surrounding me. They were all similar height and had close-cropped hair. Taking those two characteristics only, they could have passed for me.

But the men were fat. They ate cheeseburgers for breakfast, lunch, and dinner. To put it simply, the lineup was bullshit. So suggestive that Stevenson would roll over in her grave. I was the champ, and I stood out like a sore thumb here.

"Am I gonna get my waffle?" I said.

"Gedrin, one more word outta ya. Go ahead."

I stayed quiet for the time being.

"Showtime. Chin up, head up. No smiling," the warden said to the group.

We all obliged.

There was a knock from the other side of the glass.

"Right profile," the warden said.

I turned to my left and showed the right side of my body along with the other hombres. Or so I thought. One person screwed it up, and the warden snapped.

"You want the hole? Turn to your fucking left, boy."

The man righted the ship quickly.

"Left profile."

We all obliged again.

There were two knocks on the glass.

This threw the warden for a second, but then it clicked. He opened another black metal door opposite the side I came in from and disappeared.

I wanted to crack jokes about Houdini with the other fine citizens, but I didn't want to make the lineup even more suggestive. So I let it slide. Besides, the fine citizens looked like a tough crowd anyway. They were all business, no smiles staring at that glass.

The warden's voice boomed over the intercom.

"Number three, step forward."

The fine citizens remained mum. The play was clear. The screwjob would begin in earnest now. I stepped forward, and I couldn't contain myself given the circumstances. I'd done twelve fucking years for a crime I didn't commit, and I wasn't about to play patsy.

I curtsied and flexed my biceps. I moonwalked for a few steps and then took a bow in front of the glass. Then I started doing some salsa steps. I had the groove all right.

"Come forward," the warden shouted.

He was having so much fun behind the curtain.

But so was I.

"Not till I get a Belgian waffle with one-hundred-percent maple syrup," I said.

I heard groans from the fine citizens behind me. They wanted to get out and resume their banal lives, and who could blame them? But I wasn't succumbing to the masses.

I walked up to the glass and made a big palm print on it.

Before I could do a second one, the lights went off, and all was dark again.

"Walk three steps, asshole," the warden said.

"Make me," I said.

"Suit yourself."

I felt a fist knock the wind right outta me. Then two people dragged me by the arms and through what I presumed was a doorway.

The lights snapped on, and for a moment I saw the lineup room again. The fine citizens were all gone. Maybe out the back door for all their hard work. But when I shook the cobwebs off, I found myself in another interrogation room. It wasn't rooms one through four that I'd passed earlier. It was even dirtier and didn't have any tables or chairs. I was being propped up by two men in suits, and they pushed me forward.

A woman came out of the shadows. She would give Salma Hayek a run for her money any day of the week.

She leaned in and whispered in my ear.

"Gringo, why the fuck are you looking for my brother Paco?" she said.

15

I lied.

"For YouTube content creation tips," I said. "He's a natural."

The woman put her hands on her hips and pulled out a cigarette. She was wearing a dark pinstripe suit with heels, and her shirt looked like it was made from the finest of Egyptian silks. She took a drag and blew the smoke right in my face.

I was partially asthmatic, so if there was anything I despised more than assholes, it was carcinogenic assholes.

"Blow your fucking dust at the warden," I said.

The woman slapped me in the face.

"He's too nice," she said.

I felt the burn sink in, but was more interested in who in the blue hell this lady was.

She walked around the empty room and examined its unfinished walls. She ran her hands down some of the corners and then examined her fingers. The look on her face said she was expecting dust, but she came away demoralized and empty-handed. She came back to the center of the room and took another drag on her cigarette.

"Paco is on a special project, understand? He's been working on it for quite some time. Leave him be. His name carries a lot of sway around here. He's not all tires, gringo. The last thing my family needs is some pendejo coming in here and ruining what we've worked for."

She walked closer to me, and I noticed her fragrance for the first time. She was a Dior woman, through and through. The smoke took a bit off the perfume, but it was there.

"Lo siento," I said.

I put my hands up and raised my brows.

The woman laughed like one of those clowns at a clown show.

"Gringo, you have a very good accent."

"Gracias."

"De nada. But don't let my sympathies fool you. Josita holds just as much sway in the family as my stupid brother."

She took another drag on her cigarette.

"Bueno," I said. "You're scoring points. Macho put that poor javelina in the road. The bastard."

Josita blew more smoke in my face. I wanted to give her a right uppercut, but I let it pass.

"My brother is an interesting man," she said. "I cannot speculate what he does in his off hours. But gringo, everything he does has a purpose. He doesn't forgive, and he sure as hell doesn't forget. I don't know if he's fond of javelinas, or any animals for that matter, but that action wouldn't surprise me in the slightest. Papa used to say that Paco was a very special boy. He'd be king one day. Such was his effect."

Josita looked at the suits as she spoke, and it didn't take a rocket scientist to figure out that she really called the shots. Not that asshole Macho. But a front is a front and a captive had no choice but to take it all in.

I closed my eyes for a second, not so much because I was figuring out my next move, but to rest them. The course had done a number on me this morning. When I opened them, Josita was looking at the walls again.

She turned back toward me. I didn't know which way the conversation would swing, but I was ready for all outcomes. If this was an amicable discourse between a champ and a player in a big illicit enterprise, so be it. If it was a pathetic attempt to lull me close, keep my guard down, and attack, well, I'd beat the shit out of the wannabe guards faster than you could say pancakes.

But if the warden sent in reinforcements, that's when things would get tricky. I liked my odds against all comers, but math doesn't lie sometimes. I scanned the space and knew that I needed to stir the pot.

To escape the hell out of Dodge.

Where you're going, there ain't no bail. My time was running out.

"Get me outta here and you have a deal," I said.

Josita laughed. "I'm not making an offer, gringo."

"There's always an offer and a counteroffer. I seal these lips about that javelina, and you get me back to Henri."

"He's a cute animal, isn't he?" Josita smiled, but it was so fake it'd make the celebs proud.

"Henri is an excellent citizen in a not so excellent world."

She nodded at the suits, and they closed the distance. I backed up with my hands up, keeping them in my sights. Two was easy-peasy.

"How stupid do you think we are?" Josita said. "We're gonna kill you in the middle of the day at a police station with all these cameras and witnesses? Estupido, worse than my brother."

I kept my fists up for a few more seconds. But the suits just stood there. No fighting stance. Nada. After about a twenty-three-second staring contest, I lowered my hands, one at a time. If the suits tried anything I'd have no problem getting back to my guard.

Josita finished her cigarette and tossed it on the ground. She stubbed it with her toe and kicked it in a corner, leaving remnants of soot on the floor.

"Deals are the work of the demonio," she said. "We have our eyes and ears on you at all times. Comprendes?" Her accent was one of the sexiest I'd ever heard. Behind her eyes I could see the trials and tribulations she'd gone through to get to the top. It was lonely at the top, but damn was it powerful. She hadn't gotten there by doing favors.

I put my fists up to fight, then lowered them, laughing at the suits.

"You don't pay these pendejos enough," I said.

"They do quite well for themselves."

Yep.

"The S-class is shit," I said. "One gasket blows and adios amigos with that green."

Josita smiled. "My Mercedes is much better than Paco's."

She walked up to me, stopping less than an arm's length away.

"Do we have an understanding, gringo?"

She ran her hands down the small of my back, then down the front of my body. I was angry, but I was also turned on, which was never a good combo. I closed my eyes and smiled again.

She blew one last puff of smoke in my face, and I could feel all the carcinogens feasting on my skin.

Then she kneed me in the balls.

"You fuck around with my family, your cojones will be the least of your worries. I have all the javelinas in the world, gringo."

She pulled a knife out of her pocket and sliced my forearm. It was a small cut, by design, but my body didn't know the difference. Blood poured out of the wound and spotted the floor.

The suits laughed, and just like that they poured out of the room.

I stayed where I was, holding my bruised jewels. It took several minutes for the pain to subside and the fog to clear. When it did, I took my shirt off and used it as a bandage for my arm.

I had more questions than answers now. Macho's special project was my special project, and I'd find it come hell or high water. Fuck with the sleuth and you get the horns.

The door banged hard.

"Showtime," the warden said.

16

I never got my Belgian waffle, but I got a ride back to the badminton club. The warden blasted some country drawl on the way there, snapping his fingers to the beat and scowling at all the slowpokes on the road. I was tempted to talk sports with the dude to kill the time, but I let it be. Despite the Suns cap on his dashboard, I didn't want to give him any reason to prolong the ride and re-think his decision to cut me loose. Josita might have called the shots in the room, but the warden called them out on the road. And he wouldn't hesitate to fuck with me again in a heartbeat.

I closed my eyes and tried to get some shuteye. It was futile because I was allergic to cop cars, and the warden's steering left much to be desired. I rubbed my eyes and then stared out the window. Ten minutes later we were back at the club. The warden parked in the lone handicapped spot and got out. He took his sweet ole time getting to the door. When he opened it, he smirked.

"Fooled me once, ain't gonna happen again, you hear? The pretty lady doesn't mince words, champ."

"Pretty indeed."

The warden undid my cuffs and I got out of the car. It was his last bit of control, holding me in the damned things till the last possible moment. A sane lawman would have let me chill, but wardens operated differently in New Mexico I guess.

He dusted some soot off his shirt, hopped back in his car, flicked me off, and was gone.

I was free.

And Henri was waiting.

I walked back into the club and found the playroom. When I'd first left him in there, he had been surrounded by six other canines, and he'd jumped right into the fray, playing chase and fetch and having a blast. Now, the poor chap was lying on the ground, spent. Hattie was trying to play tug-of-war with him, but he wasn't having it. Some other canines tried to nudge him to join the party, and Henri completely ignored their overtures.

"I thought you died," Hattie said.

"I spent several hours in jail," I said.

Hattie laughed. "You're something else, you know that?"

I told her again because honesty is the best policy sometimes. She still didn't buy it.

"Mister, you owe me an Uber back."

"Didn't you hustle the taquito man?"

Hattie rolled her eyes. "I did, but then I got stiffed. In front of all his cronies."

"The security bitch too?"

"Yeah, he told everybody else not to pay out."

"I should have taken him when I had the chance. Shown him some manners," I said.

Hattie punched me in the shoulder, as nicely as possible. I let her.

"Cute, but I'm not that kind of girl."

She took the tug rope from Henri's mouth and threw it

toward the back of the play area. Three cocker spaniels who'd just been admitted to the fun fest got there first. Henri looked confused for a second, then he hobbled over to them and let out a growl, and one of them dropped the rope. He didn't pick it up. He just lay down next to a Maltese mix.

"Damn, he is quite the service dog," Hattie said.

"Henri picks it up in the later rounds. He's a slow starter sometimes."

Hattie laughed. "Tell that to the four squeaky toys he broke today. The front desk almost made me pay for the damages."

I smiled, then I called Henri. He got up and sprinted to my side. He was back. We walked out of the place, and Hattie played with her phone while we waited for our ride. I was a chivalrous man, so I'd booked the Uber this time. A part of me wanted to keep Hattie around in my orbit, but another part of me wanted to know where in the blue hell Macho was. What was he hiding? Why did he have his sister do his dirty work?

The fact that Josita wanted to play hardball made *me* wanna play hardball. That's the way it works in this business. Find a clue. Keep on digging. Bigger and better and faster. Add it all up, and bingo.

Macho and the watch were connected. And so was my dad. I was sure of it.

I looked over at Hattie, and she was scratching Henri's whiskers. The rascal didn't take to just anybody, so the fact that he was cool with Hattie was a very good sign indeed.

"What?" Hattie said.

She'd caught me.

"Nada."

"Didn't look like nada, you stalker."

"I wanted a dose of fresh air, and your direction seems to have provided it."

The gears were churning in Hattie's head, but she didn't say anything after that.

Our Uber came and we all hopped in. I was grateful to learn that this was not an experiment, and the apparatus would be completely human-operated this time. My bowels were thankful too.

Hattie told the driver where the shop was, and we all settled in. I looked out my window at nothing in particular, and Hattie eyed the driver's speedometer.

"Chillax, you stalker," I said.

Hattie laughed.

"His check engine light is on. So many possible causes for that. Maintenance is like sex: the more you do it, the better off you'll be."

I had about a hundred witty responses to that, but I went minimalist.

"Si."

Hattie didn't let me off that easy.

"You got a bunch of ladies, huh, champ? I see how it is."

"My mistress is the law and my lady is Aunt Jemima. Best damned syrup in the world."

"You know she got canceled, right? And it's filled with high-fructose."

I had no idea what the hell Hattie was talking about. Then she explained it in full. Apparently certain images rubbed people the wrong way. The thought of a syrup bottle getting canceled made my stomach boil. The cancel hombres had gone too far this time. I was all about the taste and the tradition of a top-notch breakfast. High-fructose be damned. I vowed to stock up on Aunt Jemima's if I found any stray bottles on the way to Old Faithful.

We sat in silence for a few minutes. The driver wasn't in the mood for small talk either, so he blasted his music. I placed it as some kind of Mediterranean mix, but I was too tired to figure it out.

Somewhere in between the driver blasting the music and us reaching our destination, Hattie took my hand. It wasn't obvious at first, but then it was. Her left hand fit my right hand like a glove. She caressed my knuckles and didn't make eye contact. I could have put a stop to it right then and there, but I enjoyed every second of it. I wanted it to keep going. And so it did. Hattie caressed my hand and inched her body closer and closer to me.

Until her thighs were touching mine.

Henri must have really liked her, because he didn't do anything.

"Let's grab a real drink tonight," she said. "My place at eight."

I thought about it for a moment. Having random activities on the night of my speech would certainly derail things, not to mention the fact that I still was on a mission.

I politely declined and asked to reschedule.

Hattie took it all in stride.

She ran her hand down the small of my back, then proceeded toward the front of my thighs. I was ticklish, and she knew it. She was having a blast.

I leaned in, trying to lessen some of the tickles. Then she kissed me. Full-on French style. I let it slide the first few seconds. She was upping the ante, not me. I was simply here with Henri, trying to accomplish a variety of tasks before midnight.

But sometimes the little head is smarter than the big head.

I kissed her back.

We took turns. Henri was super chill, but the driver wasn't.

"Nothing on my seats, dammit. Please."

"Most def, breh," I said.

We took more turns. They say clarity is a byproduct of all that oxytocin.

I broke away first.

"Where's Macho's place?" I said.

"Why?" Hattie said.

"I don't wanna go to yours yet."

17

Macho was a god. Twenty-foot wrought-iron gates lined the perimeter of his place and those who dared climb to the skies would be greeted with spiky shards at the top. The more clever folk who tried to hop the corners would find gargantuan stone lion heads staring right at their pupils.

I didn't see Josita or her cronies anywhere in sight, but the message was clear: the owner of this swanky abode didn't play.

"Let's go," Hattie said.

She beckoned me back to the Uber, but I was just getting started. I walked along the fence, looking for any chink in the armor. But the gates were solid grade, and it didn't take me long to realize that my efforts were futile.

No wonder there wasn't a security hombre anywhere in sight.

After another minute of examining the fortress, Hattie got out of the Uber, and it sped away.

She pretended to care about the fence, then walked over to me.

"I miss that Uber," I said.

"I miss a lot more than that Uber," she said.

We shared a smile, then we both gazed at Macho's place. It was definitely new construction. Probably right after his tire tricks saturated all of social media. But all was fair in the celeb game. I'd seen dudes spend more money on their toilet paper rack than the average person spent on a whole kitchen.

If Macho went big on the outside, the inside would be ten times as big. Men like Macho couldn't bear to finish second in anything. The taquito man had all but confirmed it. Macho was all image, all the time. He couldn't disclose his sexuality to the world, and he sure as hell couldn't disclose that he lived below his station.

I pegged Macho's interior as Scandinavian deco style. That would hit all the right spots for his ilk.

"No late-night rendezvous at the big house?" I said to Hattie.

She rolled her eyes.

"Fat chance. He's the biggest prick when it comes to his female employees. Only reason I got hired in the first place was because my ass was there before his ass took over. I was at headquarters from day one."

"I must confess, your ass is much better."

I grinned, and Hattie took my hand again.

We walked around the perimeter of the property. I couldn't spot any cameras, but if people could order rides from a phone nowadays, they could easily make cameras like breadcrumbs and stick them anywhere. We were surely being watched. But the more the merrier. Maybe I'd get to meet the staff properly and explain my purpose. I just wanted to ask the tire don a question. Simple as that. Questions made the world go round, and there were never any stupid questions.

Hattie pointed to a dilapidated security booth on the southwest corner. A back road tailed off into the distance.

"Big bucks," I said.

"Whatever," Hattie said.

Macho might have been a mega-success now, but given his lowly auto boy beginnings, it made sense to keep some of the old despite the new. I could see a garage off in the distance, and I could picture Macho working on some big techie cars in peace and solitude. With all the security around the place, nobody would dare interrupt his activities.

Except for a boxing champ with only a smidge of brain cells left.

I started walking down the back road, but Hattie stopped me.

"Push it," she said.

She pointed to a button right below the booth. It looked rusted from years of inactivity. Maybe Macho hadn't gotten around to replacing all the old after all.

I looked through the fence. I wanted to push the button, but I also wanted to ensure that I wouldn't be ravaged by some very unfriendly canines hiding behind the walls.

I slowly moved my hand toward the button and when I got within inches of it, I paused.

"Where's Henri?" I said.

The rascal had gotten out of the Uber with Hattie but was now camouflaging himself somewhere.

"A service companion always waits for his owner to inspect the premises," Hattie said. She was spot-on with my accent, and I appreciated the call-back. But still, I wanted Henri by my side so he could take any other possible canines to school.

I told Henri to come, but I was met with nothing but the sound of the wind blowing through the tree branches above the booth.

Hattie whistled, and I heard the monster before he made the turn around the corner. He was drooling like a boss and had a wide smile on his face.

"Damn," I said.

"Fun fact: I was a dog trainer in Fresno for a while."

"A woman with many talents. I dig that."

"Indeed."

Before I could be even wittier, she pressed the button below the booth.

Nada.

She pressed it again.

Nada.

She punched it a third time, and for a second I thought I heard nada, but then there was static. A few seconds later an old lady's voice crackled on the other end of the line.

"Who this?" the old lady said.

"Macho macho macho," I said.

Hattie punched me in the shoulder.

There was a long pause on the other end of the line.

"Idiota," she said. "Macho no esta aqui."

Ah, there's the rub.

Macho's maid, or significant other, or whoever it was didn't speak English as her primary language. Which was great for me, because I'd resorted to Spanish as my primary language on more than one occasion. My skills were legendary.

"Donde esta?" I said.

Where is he?

More static.

"No se."

I don't know.

"Quiero hablar con el. Es muy importante."

I need to speak with him. It's very important.

The old lady demurred and kept telling me Macho wasn't

94

home. But I wasn't going to let her off that easy. I needed to look around and make my own assessment.

"Tengo empanadas," I said.

I have empanadas.

That did the trick.

The gates at the front swung open slower than molasses, and when they parted, Henri sprinted forward to all the new sights and sounds while Hattie and I dragged behind.

"Your Spanish is so sexy," Hattie said. "But you know that, obvi. It's cool, for real."

"I share the sentiment," I said.

I walked inside the gates with a pep to my step, not because of Hattie, but because I knew Henri would have dispatched any and all threats before I'd crossed the threshold.

Hattie whispered in my ear.

"What's the play?"

"Ask a question, get an answer, then ask another question."

"No shit. Seriously?"

I wanted to keep it as simple as possible. That meant finding Macho and extracting all the necessary information from his candy ass.

"A sleuth keeps on sleuthing," I said.

Hattie shook her head and found the front steps first. I'd expected a pool and slabs of marble leading to a big-ass door fit for a castle. Instead, the layout was rather basic, at least on this side. A cobblestone pathway led to three concrete steps, followed by a large welcome mat in front of a fiberglass door.

Hattie knocked. Four slow, melodic taps. I appreciated it, and the door swung open right away.

A maid stood on the other side, and the moment she saw Hattie she rushed over and hugged her.

"Mi hija," she said. "Como estas?"

The old lady from the intercom was the maid, and the maid knew Hattie.

"Deceptive, huh, missy?" I said.

Hattie smiled. "Paco's an asshole, but she's awesome. Reminds me of my mother."

We went inside, and that's when the opulence of the place really hit its mark. Marble columns supported tall ceilings that flanked winding staircases to the upper quadrants of the home.

Sims would be proud.

I told the maid I wanted Macho. She told me he wasn't here. Then Hattie told her I wanted a grand tour, and the maid obliged.

There was an entertainment room on the first floor, five bedrooms on the second, and a gym on the third. I hadn't seen a single bathroom, but I figured Macho had them on the fourth. When we got to the gym, Hattie took the maid to the side and started whispering things to her, like old friends catching up. Then she looked over at me and gave me a look that said *go for it, hombre.*

The minute she walked down the hall with the maid, I went back down to the second level and looked for Macho. I pulled open all the closets and looked under all the beds. I cracked open all the windows and peeked out at the balconies.

I saw Henri playing by the cobblestone, but that's all she wrote.

No Macho.

I went back upstairs and realized there wasn't a fourth-floor bathroom extravaganza after all. Just one. At the end of the hall was a master bath with a triple sink and box shower and a tub lined with rose petals. And I was no closer to Macho than Sal was to selling his damned gym back in Chicago.

But serendipity is real sometimes.

Hattie and the maid had arrived ahead of me, and the maid was sitting on the edge of the tub and holding her forehead.

"El jefe tiene los barcos. Pienso que allí esta. No dormí aqui anoche."

The boss has boats. I think he's there. He didn't sleep here last night.

It all made sense.

"Boss man has a boat. The bastard."

Hattie rolled her eyes. "Three. He always gloats about it."

"Where's he keep them?"

Hattie pulled out her phone and showed me.

18

We found the place an hour later. It sat next to a small pond at the corner of a gravel road in the middle of nowhere. Hattie told me the name multiple times on the ride over, but I quickly forgot it. The storage facility was surrounded by steel fencing that made Macho's lions look like chump change, and the sign out front welcoming the masses had so much dirt on it I couldn't spell a damned word.

If I had to put a number on it, the facility held three hundred boats easy, nestled among multiple levels of storage. There were three levels, and each boat was on wheels, surrounded by globs of chains. Part security, part convenience for the owners. Unlock the chains in a jiffy, attach the boats to a rig, and find the high seas.

A sign at the front desk read, "Back in 15 minutes. Be kind to your fellow boater!" I walked past it into the belly of the place, and realized that each level represented a hierarchy of sorts. The boats on the bottom were the entry-level boats. Small slips that high schoolers would party on with their friends during spring break. The middle tier were the tweeners. The top was the cream of the crop. Gargantuan yachts that stretched to the sky.

I doubted that the owners on the top levels got their boats out that much. A rusty freight elevator sat opposite the nearest boat, at least fifty yards away, and if there was anything I'd learned about those in the top stations of life, it was that petty inconveniences got under their skin like a fly on a hot summer's day. That, and given their station, their boats here were probably backups. The big kahunas were already out on the waters.

But we were close.

I knew Macho's boat was on that top level, but Hattie wanted to start on the bottom.

"He only has one of them here," she said. "He wouldn't shut up about it on his lunch breaks."

"And the other two are in another palace?" I said.

"Storage. The cheap-ass kind," she said. "He might know a little about tires, but he knows jack shit about boats. I don't think he can even drive the damned thing."

"A man of many talents is very hard to find."

"I'll say."

She smiled, ran her fingers through her hair, then walked past me real slow, looking back over her left shoulder. Ah, the beauty of the female sex. While my track record was the worst of all time, I admired the female sex the way Henri admired a couple of steaks.

And that would never go out of style.

"Vamos," I said.

I followed Hattie and counted the boats as I passed. Six, seven, eight. They were all white, and they were all in various states of disrepair. But they had clearly been put to the test far more often than some of the bigger wares in the place. The high schoolers enjoyed mudding.

We trudged on, and soon Henri caught up to us. He'd been sniffing the fence, and now he proceeded to sniff every boat. The rascal was loving life, and I was loving having him by my side. Sharing all these experiences with him was a beautiful thing, and man's best friend wasn't a misnomer by any means.

Hattie came up empty on the first level, so we went up a few spiral steps and found the second level. The boats here looked like they'd avoided the mud a tad bit more, but they were still in disarray. I spotted a broken rudder, a broken sail, and a spare engine that looked yellower than pirate teeth.

"My dinero is on *Casa de Macho*," I said.

"What?" Hattie said.

"The name. Of the boat."

She punched me in the shoulder. "You really don't stop, do you?"

"I can go all night if I have to."

"We'll see about that."

We shared another look and walked on. The tension was real, and the hormones didn't lie. I knew where this was headed. The question was, did I want to go down that road again? Both my heads were taking sides.

Oh well.

"How many knockouts do you have?" Hattie asked.

She was placing her hands on the boats as she passed, inspecting them for who knows what.

I'd never been asked that question before and was thrown off for a minute. The average hombre on the street would get all giddy about how I knocked the shit out of so-and-so, in such-and-such fight, at such-and-such venue, but they never cared about the actual numbers. The nitty-gritty was usually left to the boxing historians and the promoters. The fans would just as soon ditch me for another knockout artist to suit their viewing pleasures.

So Hattie had a technical question, and a technical question required a technical answer. I loved technicalities, but the truth was I had no fucking idea how many knockouts I had. Sal had probably forgotten a third of them by now, but Sims probably carried them on a piece of paper somewhere.

I lied for the first time with Hattie.

"Seventy-three," I said.

She rolled with it and was quite impressed. She took my hand and we went up to the third level. I didn't complain one bit. Support was always nice for all those steps.

There were just four boats on the third level. Seeing as they were the cream of the crop, this made perfect sense. All the boats had been used and maintained properly over the years. Not a single streak of mud or rust on them. The big boys didn't play when it came to cleanliness on the water, and they seemed to take just as much pride when storing their toys.

Henri went to work first. His average sniff time was ten seconds on level one. On the second level his average went up to thirteen, and now he kept it at a solid eleven seconds for the first three boats. Sniff, wag tail, on to the next.

The fourth boat was different.

Henri sniffed for thirty-three seconds, and his tail wagged faster than you could say hola. He whined repeatedly, and I knew we'd hit jackpot.

I pulled back the tarp on the boat and hopped on with Hattie. Henri didn't need an invitation, but he stayed outside the boat running back and forth, whining louder and louder.

"He got fed in the playroom," Hattie said.

I nodded. "Henri believes in strenuous cardio at multiple intervals throughout the day."

Hattie walked along the side deck of the boat. "What kind of treasure are we looking for?" she said.

"The big kind," I said.

Truth be told, I was still figuring out why the hell we were here. Yes, this was where Macho's boat was, but in the bigger picture I had no idea where all this was leading. Macho could have been anywhere in the world right now. Still, this was part and parcel of the amateur sleuth game: coming up flummoxed and regrouping to get to the bottom of it. Find something and keep plugging away. I had to see this through. Josita and company could go fuck themselves.

I didn't play.

I looked around the boat and saw a cooler, a life vest, and more.

Much more.

Watches.

The asshole had about twenty different timepieces sprawled out near the cockpit. Seikos, Rolexes, Omega, Citizen, Breitling. Macho was a damned catalog for the nouveau riche.

I took the Breitling in my hands and analyzed its fine craftsmanship. Then Hattie poked me on the shoulder.

"Someone's on the boat," she whispered.

I immediately put my fists up, ready to throw down. When you're a professional brain basher your antennas never go out of service. But this wasn't a street fight or even a boxing match.

I spotted something far tamer below the cockpit of the boat. A lady sitting on a makeshift bed.

If I had to guess her profession I'd say she was a hooker. I had antennas for that kind of thing too.

As soon as I took a step below deck, the hooker started crying.

"I killed him. I couldn't help it."

She didn't even turn to greet me.

19

The hooker was wearing a thin green skirt over fishnet leggings. The tats on her calves were so big they screamed out even over the cheetah-print platform booties. I couldn't make out the designs, though I tried. On top, she wore a white crop top with no bra underneath and a fake necklace she'd probably gotten from a mall somewhere.

I had hooker game, but I didn't have therapy game. The hooker kept crying. In between her sniffles she wiped her nose and mumbled words.

"I killed him by having standards. He wanted to have fun, and I wanted fancy dinners and cozy nights by the fire. I was done with this life, but he wasn't. I drove him away and now he's all gone. He's never coming back."

She still hadn't turned to face me or Hattie. She was sitting on the edge of the bed and rocking back and forth.

In these types of situations, a feminine touch begets a feminine touch. A little bit of estrogen goes a long way. I looked to Hattie for salvation, but she was just as confused as I was. She stared at the hooker with furrowed brows, and for a moment I thought Hattie was gonna give her a left hook straight to the right earlobe. That, or lecture her on how she needed to suck it up and stop being so reliant on the male sex.

Nada.

But service dogs come in handy sometimes too. They possess all the skills that humans don't. They have a delicate touch, and their actions speak far louder than words.

Henri went up to the hooker and started licking her legs. At first the hooker didn't notice. She kept crying and sniffling and rocking on the bed. But Henri was determined. He hopped up on the bed and started licking her neck, and when that didn't work he burrowed his head into the hooker's lap and left it there.

She caved.

She rubbed Henri's head and held him very tight. She paused like that for a long beat, Henri being a trooper the whole way through. And finally she stood from the bed and turned around. She looked like a smoker who had gotten tired of smoking.

"Sorry," she said.

"Take all the time you need," Hattie said.

"What she said," I said.

We all stood there looking for the next line. I wanted more info on Macho, but I also wanted to be delicate a little while longer, lest the hooker dive back into hysterics.

I examined more of the boat for show, then Hattie broke the silence.

"When did you last see him?"

The hooker looked like she was gonna cry again, then she got serious.

"Yesterday that damned Paco was gonna take me out. Got all dressed up nice and the whole works. Just when I was ready to show off these assets, he says he's got a meeting, but we can go on the boat for a little bit and fool around."

The hooker scratched Henri's whiskers as she was talking.

"This boat and with that Paco?" I said. I pictured Fester.

"This old thing barely kicks out on the lake. He took me once, and I was holding on for dear life. Good Lord. His other one. He docks it outside. The same Paco, handsome."

Interesting.

"Boats are it," she said. "Lot of memories on them boats. So we go out on the water, and before you know it there ain't much talking going on, if you know what I mean. That's how he wanted it."

I was smiling, and Hattie snapped me out of it.

The hooker knew her effect though, and she returned the smile.

"What else?" Hattie said.

"The marine club is fine and dandy. Been a member many times, but then Paco told me to get lost. He was never late to meetings, and he wasn't about to start then. He took that boat for a spin, dropped me off at the docks, and that's about it." She looked me up and down. "Honey, you look familiar."

"I'm perhaps the world's most famous nomad," I said.

I could see the gears churning in her head, but the hooker didn't come back with a witty reply. Instead, she held out her paw for Henri, and he took it like a champ. She laughed.

"The asshole hasn't answered my calls or texts since," she said. "I came back here hoping to find his ass. When he'd have a bender he'd find his way out here. Away from the wifey. He was gonna get a divorce. He promised me."

Hattie rolled her eyes.

I said nothing.

When the hooker was done with her spiel I asked her where the lake was.

"It started with 'C,'" she said. "I don't know them lakes that well, honey. So many of them out in these here parts. Ask me about the bayou and I can tell you every rhyme and verse down there. So long as the company's good, that's all that matters, honey."

She eyed me seductively again, and I followed suit. Acting was quite fun sometimes.

Hattie stepped between us. "What's his business, exactly?"

The hooker held up her hands. "Business is business. I never ask a man his business. Maybe that's why I kept him this long."

She sat back down on the bed and took a long look around at the remnants of her dalliances with Macho. Some called it fucking, others called it casual, and others called it hanging out. The world was an interesting place. Bottom line, the hooker felt like she had a heart of gold and was scorned. I was wondering how Macho got it up if he played the other side of the fence, but there were more pressing matters.

Why keep the watches on the boat?

I racked my brain for the answer, but then Hattie tapped me on the shoulder.

"Got it."

She showed me a musty map she'd snagged from abovedeck. It wasn't quite atlas-size, but it did the trick.

She splayed the map out on the bed and began pointing at random things. She gestured wildly as she did this, and I found myself mesmerized. She was sexy as hell. In that moment it was just us on that boat. The hooker forgotten.

I didn't want a relationship per se. I seldom achieved success in that department. But a man has needs, and a woman does too. Many a time those needs are mutual and they align perfectly.

I took her hand and squeezed it.

"Y'all are cute," the hooker said.

"He's an asshole sometimes, but we'll figure it out," Hattie said.

I stayed quiet.

She pulled out a pen and circled a spot on the map. She said the name a couple times, but I forgot it.

The hooker sat back down on the bed, and Henri started licking her again. I gave Henri the "off" command and he was spot-on. Hattie gave him a treat, and then we bounced outta Dodge faster than you could say Dodge.

But first we had to deal with the storage manager.

20

The hooker and I got the boat out on the water. The storage manager had made us fill out some forms before taking the monstrosity out of storage, but we'd managed, and we'd unloaded it at one of the off ramps at Cochiti Lake. It was roughly fifty miles upstream from Albuquerque and it had some beautiful ambience. The hooker's part was supposed to end there, but she wanted closure, and Hattie felt for her in some strange way. So she joined us on the water.

I wanted to test my nautical skills, so I took the wheel. I had no idea what I was doing, but Hattie apparently had driven a boat before so she started barking orders from jump street.

The boat glided on the water so easily I thought I was walking on air. The rudder made some wretched noises at the start, but after the first couple minutes on the water it was clear sailing. The summer sun shone in the distance, and as I looked out over the lake at the other boats flanking us, I realized the party was just getting started. There were less than a couple hours of daylight left on this summer night, but the kegs and red cups and beer pong contraptions were out in full force. I spied twenty-three coeds getting their groove on, and for a moment I was tempted to join in on the fun.

A blondie with an American-flag-themed bikini curled her fingers in my direction in a *come hither* motion. I played it cool, but then she did it again, and I couldn't control myself.

"Pull the stern ten knots left," I said.

Hattie smacked me across the top of the head.

"You're not helping yourself, carless wonder."

"Indeed."

I felt the back of my skull for any damage, and after being satisfied there was nada, I looked back at the blondie.

But she was gone. Off to greener pastures with a bleached-blonde quarterback who waxed his chest. Ah, the insanity.

I stayed steady at the wheel and picked up speed with the boat. I felt myself gradually leaning back in my seat. Henri barked at some of the ripples on the water, and then started chasing his tail for a bit. I appreciated the entertainment.

I looked out over the horizon and saw small shapes in the distance. I couldn't tell what they were, but my mind was telling me it was Macho playing games. Maybe he was on a boat swinging a deal, or maybe he was on another boat "banging" a different hooker. Whatever the hell the asshole was doing, he was mine. I'd been chasing him all day, and at the end of the day games were games. Games get old, and when they get old, somebody has to pay the price. Macho was going to get his ass kicked for ruining my round of golf. All I'd wanted was to shoot a kickass score, enjoy a little bit of the great state of New Mexico, and give my speech tonight.

But the best-laid plains go awry far more often than expected. First the watch fiasco, and now the quasi-disappearance act with his cartel wannabe sister, Josita. Macho was leaving little nuggets, but I was running around in circles chasing a dude who didn't deserve to be chased.

A part of me wanted to just call it quits and go give my speech and move on to my next adventure. Old Faithful wasn't going anywhere. But curiosity killed the cat. That summed up my life in a myriad of ways. Once I had something in my mind, it remained fixed there like Gorilla Glue.

I knew exactly what I was going to do to Macho when I found him. Damned near down to the nittiest, grittiest detail. I'd take my fists and bend his skull. I'd fuck up his nose and make his mouth spew all sorts of languages. I'd cap it all off with a boot to the balls.

But that'd be letting him off too easy. Hell, I'd make him watch my speech with Henri tonight too. I'd tape him all back together again, and I'd seat him in the front row where all the top animal peeps were. I'd give him a nice suit for the occasion. I'd smile and say all the right lines at all the right times. Henri would bark on cue and perform a bunch of tricks for the masses.

Then the show would be over, and I'd get what I wanted.

An "I fucked up" straight from Macho's mouth. An apology of epic proportions. The full scoop on my dad and his watch and how it got in his pudgy-ass hands. Then I'd take him out back, undo the wrappings, and pound the shit out of him worse than I did that dude with the brass knucks way back when.

And just like that it'd be all over. The synapses in my brain could recalibrate and relax. Therapeutic release was muy bueno.

But it wasn't that easy. It seldom was in this world. Something tugged at the back of my skull. Was my dad still out there somewhere? Beating the shit out of Macho was fine and dandy, but what if he could lead me to my pops? I'd never believed the story that he washed away at sea. It was too cinematic to be based in any part of reality. Where in the blue hell did he wash away? What were the damned coordinates? What time of day was it? Who was present for the lost-at-sea portion of the narrative?

Mama Gedrin had been short on the details with me growing up, and it reeked of a coverup. Not from my mama, but from those who played the strings.

I'd carried this burden on my shoulders my whole life. It weighed me down like a million sandbags. I never got to play catch with my old man, or grab hot dogs at the ball park, or get the birds and the bees speech.

I'd turned out all right, but maybe I was the exception to the rule.

I squeezed the life out of the steering wheel and the boat stayed the course. My mind kept firing on all cylinders. On the one hand I was logical, and on the other hand I was diabolical. Was I just as fucked up as the rest of the bad hombres I'd dealt with in this world? Did I need changing in this greater landscape around me? The closer I got to finding what I was looking for, the further away I truly felt.

I couldn't hold a relationship and I beat people's brains for a living. The squared circle wasn't all it was shaped up to be sometimes.

Henri groaned, and when I looked back, Hattie was rubbing his belly. The rascal had it made.

I laughed. And then the hooker spoiled the party.

"We did dust right up here," she said. We drove past a stray boat with no keg fun on it and she pointed to a clear space that wrapped swiftly around a bunch of pinyon pines. They were fine-looking things, and the bend was a secluded portion on the lake, abutted by a few single-family homes.

It made sense. Macho's activities on the water mirrored his own inner ethos. Clandestine and away from prying eyes. I wouldn't put it past Macho to be dealing on the waterways of New Mexico too. Go big or go home, hombre.

As I drove through the area, I didn't see any more boats on the water. They were either tethered to their docks or out to play somewhere else. The boat kept gliding, following the trail. We were like a serpent now, following the zigs and the zags till we found the prize. While my plan if I found Macho wasn't a surprise, I wondered what the hooker had in store for him. Maybe the hooker could throw a mean hook. Ha ha.

Then Henri barked, and I saw a cluster of small white boats. They were spread across the water in a 'Q' shape—all of them in a circle, with one boat going up to each boat around the edge and having a short discussion before proceeding to the next.

Henri barked again.

He wasn't stupid. He wasn't barking at the people, or the boats. He was barking at all the aromas that were filtering through his nose. Henri could spot a drug deal a mile away. I'd confirmed it at one of his obedience classes once.

These assholes were dealing on the water. If Macho was doing business with them, I wanted to ask them a few questions. I could spot a con faster than you could say con.

I drove past the swirl of boats, and as we passed, all the dudes instinctively looked up from whatever the hell they were doing and gave us the evil eye.

They knew what was up.

Their party was spoiled.

And I wouldn't let them forget it.

I told the hooker to grab the wheel. She hesitated for a moment, then I flashed my pearly whites and she ultimately sided with me.

"Honey, don't do anything funny now," she said.

"Amicable interactions would be best," Hattie said.

"I'll see what I can do."

We pulled up next to the boat that was going up to all the

other boats. We were inches away now, and our boat was dwarfed by the other dude's boat big-time.

I'd have to earn it. I forgot to stretch, but sometimes surprises are the best medicine. I jumped onto the other dude's boat, and I stuck the landing. The dude had a terrified look on his face.

"Where the fuck is Macho?" I said.

I gave *him* the evil eye this time.

Nada.

Then I heard the engines of all the other boats rev up. I was surrounded ten seconds later.

"Who the fuck are you?" the dude said. He'd found his courage in numbers.

"Your pussy's keeper," I said.

The dude charged, just like I'd planned it.

Showtime.

21

I've had the privilege of beating brains in on a whole variety of surfaces.

Asphalt.

Concrete.

Rubber.

Grass.

Laminate.

Plank.

But on a boat rocking on the water?

Never.

This presented a variety of challenges. First, keeping my balance among the shifting tides. Second, finding my target. Third, avoiding becoming the target. The reality was that with each rocking of the boat back and forth came the possibility of a big miss. A big miss meant leaving myself open for just a split second.

That's all a professional fighter needs to get the job done.

But luckily for me, I wasn't dealing with professionals on Cochiti Lake. Hell, *I* was the damned professional, and I'd planned this set piece out beforehand. My mind had played the movie through before I'd even jumped on the boat. I was the Oscar-winning director, and I wasn't about to cede my crown.

I knew all the ins and outs of the fight game. Prizefight or street fight. It all was the same shit. Same players and same results. I knew exactly when to start a ruckus, and you bet your ass I knew how to finish one. The game was scripted, and I knew every line like the back of my hand.

First cometh the scared one.

Check. The dude who had confidence in numbers charged me. I sidestepped him and elbowed him into next week, flinging him off the boat and into the lake.

Next cometh the wannabe hard ones.

Check. Two dudes in cargo shorts and muscle tees pulled out bats from their boats. They smiled crookedly, hopped on the first dude's boat, and closed around me. I heard Henri barking, but my mind was focused on the task at hand.

The dude in the green muscle tee swung the bat and hit air. On the recoil, I grabbed the bat and punched him in the stomach with it. His ribs crunched and started singing all sorts of songs. He keeled over, and I kicked him off the boat.

The dude in the red muscle tee got me in the ankle with a shot. He didn't connect square with the bat, but pain shot up through my body like I was on speed. A bat is a fucking bat. It wasn't the first and certainly wouldn't be the last time my brain would be sending signals of distress.

The dude swung the bat again. This time I ducked, making him hit air. I got him with a body shot, and he stumbled backward. I heard Hattie saying something, but focus is part and parcel of the fight game. A fighter who loses focus might as well choose a new profession. All it takes is a fraction of a second. The dude swung for the fences and missed widely.

I threw a right hook and he slipped it.

Left hook.

Slipped it.

Right uppercut.

Rolled out of the way.

Damn, he had game. I had to give props to the dude. He could hang a bit longer than the rest. But pride cometh before the fall.

I faked a jab and the dude covered up, just like any fighter with a semblance of a brain would do. Then he lowered his hands to fighting stance again. Just like any fighter would do. He was on autopilot. The mind-muscle connection is a beautiful thing.

But every hombre possesses different skills.

While the red muscle tee dude took a second to get his hands down, I needed even less to get my shot in.

A millisecond to be exact.

I got him with a nice jab and he started wobbling.

"You dealing the weak shit out here or the real shit?" I said.

The dude tried to throw some kicks, but I'd had enough. I threw my favorite combo.

Right cross.

Left hook.

Right shot to the solar plexus.

I would have thrown his ass into the water too, but the dude did it for me. He wobbled and fell backward into the lake.

Next cometh the one formidable opponent. Just when you think you've dispatched all foes, somebody always comes out of the woodwork, prolonging your day. Maybe it would be the leader or maybe it would be the dude one step below the leader, waiting for his moment.

It didn't matter.

Check.

A bodybuilder jumped onto the boat. He wore tight jeans

like me, and a Henley top. A gold chain hung around his neck with some foreign scrawl on it that I couldn't make out.

"Enough," he said. I detected an accent, but I couldn't place it.

"No comprendo," I said.

I held my hands up like the confused boxer that I was. Then I started shimmying my shoulders and dancing to an imaginary beat. I was getting bored, and life is always a tad bit more pleasurable when there's entertainment aplenty.

The bodybuilder wasn't pleased. He picked up a stray piece of wood from the boat and flung it right at my face. I ducked, but it hit the hooker on the other boat.

"Never mess with a working girl's moneymaker," I said.

I walked toward him.

"Shut the fuck up."

The bodybuilder walked toward me. And then there were two. He knew the score. Mano a mano.

No rush.

When he got within inches of me, he spit out of the corner of his mouth.

"This lake isn't for strangers," he said. "People here like them customs. Makes the world go round, boy."

"The world is a strange place indeed," I said. "It's not every day you get to meet such distinguished 'roid monsters on these hallowed waters. Don't mind me, hombre. I'm just here for a little Macho, Macho, baby."

I did another dance, and the bodybuilder clotheslined me. I wasn't expecting it, so I fell straight on my ass.

The bodybuilder wasted no time. He went right to ground and pound. I covered up and absorbed the shots with my elbows and forearms. Common sense dictated that something would have to give. Either the dude ran out of endurance or I ran out of consciousness.

It usually worked out for me in the end, so I stuck it out, taking more and more shots. Henri started barking again, and this gave me the opening I needed.

I kneed the bodybuilder in the balls. Twice. He fell off me, keeping his feet, and I kicked him in the face. It was a half-assed kick because I was still reeling from the shots, and because despite my foray into Muay Thai training here and there, I still couldn't throw a roundhouse kick for the life of me.

But a professional is still a professional, and he gets his wind back far quicker than a non-professional.

I bounced back to my feet and threw a right hook to the body, then another shot to his right ribs.

The bodybuilder staggered back, but he wasn't damaged in the slightest.

He kicked me in the front quad, and I could feel it shrivel up. A solid teep. The pain coursed through my body again, and the bodybuilder used the distraction to clip me with an elbow. And another one. He knew Muay Thai too. Far more advanced than me.

"Macho doesn't play," he said.

He flashed his pearly whites, and they were absolutely perfect. Better than mine, which was saying something. He must have had work done on them.

"I want you to ask him a question," I said.

"Yeah?"

"What color are the seashells by the seashore?"

"You're fucking done."

He charged at me, but this time I couldn't get out of the way because he dove like a linebacker off the blocks, pounding me into the back of the boat. My back felt like a freight train had said hello and goodbye a million times.

I was seeing three bodybuilders for a few seconds, then the

perfect teeth came into focus, and then I saw three body-builders again.

I spit at all three, and all three covered up. Then I saw his teeth again, and all was straight. I gave him everything I had, which in that moment wasn't saying much.

I was running out of gas.

I'd underestimated my opponent. Classic professional fucking problem.

I tried throwing a hook and then converting it to an elbow midway there, but he was ready for it. He slipped it and punched me right in the solar plexus. A dose of my own medicine. I keeled over, then got kicked in the face. I fell into the lake, and everything went black.

22

Fun fact: I can't swim for shit. Ever since I was a mini-Gedrin in floaties getting pushed down the waterslide, I'd hated the water. Chlorinated or any other variety. The feeling of liquid enveloping my epidermis was no bueno. My equilibrium would be off for hours afterward, and my ears could never quite get every last drop of water out.

I expected nothing less this time.

I had seen the bodybuilder's kick, but now I couldn't see shit. I tried opening my eyes, but they were glued shut. I thought about my mom and my dad and Sal. I couldn't go out like this, that was for damned sure. I had a reputation to uphold, dammit.

My mind urged me to get the fuck to the surface, but my body told me to chill out for a little bit. Ripples of water surrounded me, and I felt a heavy pressure move me a few inches to my right. Then the pressure went away. Then it returned. It went like that for a while, but I couldn't keep count.

I tried again with my eyes, and bingo they opened up. I

couldn't make anything out with any sort of detail, but shapes were shapes, and educated guesses were educated guesses.

The pressure I felt earlier was from the propellers of the boats. The dudes who'd kicked my ass were whirling around in circles, then bouncing. Little by little, the propellers receded into the distance, and after a few seconds all the pressure was gone.

I wanted to kick their candy asses for good this time, but I sat there lost in translation.

I would have stayed there longer, but I felt something tug my arm. I reached back to exterminate the threat, but the force was too strong, and I was pulled upward. I kicked my feet to get away from the threat, but I kept going upward, closer and closer to the surface. Maybe it wasn't such a threat after all.

Two seconds later, my head broke the surface and I coughed up so much water I could've held the Titanic in those droplets.

"Champ, you have many flaws."

The hooker was soaking wet, talking shit. I forced a smile. She guided me to the ladder on Macho's boat, then she pushed me up the first few rungs, and I did the rest.

I collapsed on the deck, and Henri was first on scene, licking me. He was enjoying this moment more than any other moment in his canine existence. He was grunting and whining and squealing.

I rubbed his whiskers, and that seemed to mellow him a bit. But I was still too spent to move.

"How fucking stupid are you?" Hattie said. "One on four?"

Her face was red and she looked like she'd been through the wringer. She furrowed her brow, and it didn't take a rocket scientist to realize that her question was one hundred percent rhetorical.

No answer needed or wanted.

But at times I was fond of disregarding social cues.

"Ain't no thing but a chicken wing," I said.

Hattie gritted her teeth, and for a moment I thought I'd get a second kick in the face for the day. But the moment passed, and she came closer, helped me up off the deck, and hugged me.

We stood there in each other's arms for a while. I didn't want it to end, and I'm sure the feeling was mutual. At some point, one of us broke away.

"Don't ever do that again," Hattie said. "There won't always be a swimmer on call to save your ass."

"True that," I said.

I pulled her close and kissed her. We took turns for a while and then called it quits. She went to the other side of the boat and engaged the hooker in conversation. I stayed put, looking out over the water. It was the perfect moment for self-reflection. The post-fight analysis was crucial. Things became clearer, but pride became bigger. In the prizefight game, Sal would go over tape in the locker room, dissecting every round. He didn't care that the fight was over, and that we could have just analyzed the tape during the next camp. He was all business, all the time. Always learning, always tinkering. There won't be a next time, boyo. Every fight could be your last. Savor it, but get your dumb ass ready.

I tried deconstructing this fight now. But the street fight analysis was different. Just me. I'd learned a lot from Sal, but I had nobody to make excuses to this time. I had been outnumbered, and I'd miscalculated. While I was comfortable with bats and a variety of other weapons, I hadn't anticipated my balance becoming an Achilles heel on the boat, and I sure as hell hadn't anticipated that some of the boaters would be able to throw down with a modicum of skill.

Ego is the bane of brilliance. But in every fight, there's always a silver lining.

Macho was close.

Otherwise the hombres on the boats wouldn't have put up such a valiant fight. They could have bounced the moment we got near, sans the theatrics. But they were protecting the asshole, and making a point.

Don't fuck with the boss.

I turned away from the water and looked over at Hattie and the hooker. They were playing with the wheel, laughing like schoolgirls. I was glad to see that the hooker was having some closure after all. Macho wasn't worth it.

I cracked my neck all sorts of ways and walked toward them.

"Who did he do dust with?" I asked the hooker.

"Nobody out here," she said.

"What about the jacked dude?"

"The one who kicked your ass?"

"That one."

The hooker laughed. "That's Jake Waldroni. Local kid who's won a lot of fitness competitions. He just comes here to get high and get some pussy. He's as dumb as a bag of rocks up there. But real good in bed."

She stuck her tongue out, and I didn't need the visual.

"He was dealing," I said. "There's a connection."

She shook her head. "Only connection here is you, sonny, causing a ruckus on the water. Word's gonna get out that this spot is all po-po'd up now. Business gonna go back in the shitter. This gonna destroy the community and now the locals gotta go get their cannabis and shit from their neighbor, who knows some other neighbor, and you know the rest. Not gonna be pure anymore. My business going down with it."

"I tossed my badge eons ago," I said.

"You still look like a trooper."

I knew she was right. I'd been mistaken for the blue many a time in my career. Part of it had to do with the fact that I played a cop on a TV show once, before I went to Pontiac. I'd played the role to perfection, but ended up quitting because it interfered with my training schedule. Of course, the other part of being mistaken had to do with the fact that I was a hardass and a wiseass the majority of the time. I fit the blue quite well, values notwithstanding.

"Where did y'all do the dust?" I said. "The exact coordinates."

I wanted it all, but I knew that was futile. Macho kicked the hooker off whenever he had his business liaisons. Finding the exact spot on the lake was like finding a needle in a haystack.

Good luck, amigo.

The hooker had no answer for me, so I stood there a few more seconds, pondering my next move.

The hooker already had hers.

"I appreciate the adventure, honey, but I have a date tonight. If my man is gonna play like that, then I'm gonna play like that too. Teach him a fucking lesson."

She went back belowdecks and started dolling herself up. She'd brought another purse and a change of clothes, and in seconds she'd managed to go from a hooker to an even better hooker.

When she was all done, she pointed to a dock across the way.

"I need a ride," she said.

"You're the driver," Hattie said.

"I can't mess up my nails. Larry likes them like this."

"Larry should buy you some fancy ones," I said.

The hooker laughed, but she didn't take the wheel. I didn't

ask any more questions. Hattie took the wheel and drove us to the dock. I wasn't in a boat-operating frame of mind.

The hooker bid us adieu and scampered off to her liaison with another rich denizen of New Mexico. Hattie re-routed the boat back the way we came. A few minutes later, she stopped the boat and we took in the view. The keg parties were far off in the distance, but the sun looked absolutely majestic.

"Finally, some peace and quiet," she said.

"Agreed," I said.

Hattie looked me up and down.

"You have to get out of these clothes, you'll catch pneumonia," she said.

I wholeheartedly agreed, but I didn't move.

Hattie accepted the challenge. She took my shirt off, and I let her.

But I accepted the challenge too. I took hers off.

We went down into the cabin below and took turns with the rest of our fabrics.

Then we fucked.

23

The afterglow was real. Hattie whispered sweet nothings in my ear, and I whispered sweet nothings in hers. She rubbed my left shoulder, and I rubbed her right cheek. She chuckled when she smiled, and I squinted my eyes when I flashed my pearly whites. It went like that for a few minutes, and then she turned her back to me, and I understood completely.

I pulled her close and we cuddled. She had small, shallow breaths, while mine were far deeper. I was in solid shape for my age, but cardio activities came in all shapes and sizes. This one in particular always had a penchant for revving me up.

I closed my eyes and said nothing. It was just the rhythm of our chests for a while. I had no idea what was next, and I didn't really give a shit. Oxytocin is the best medicine sometimes. Skin-on-skin contact with a beautiful woman is one of the grandest gifts of them all.

I still doubted the love parabola would end up in our favor this time, but in that moment I rolled with it and pretended to be the biggest optimist. I took my crookeds with the straights, and one day hoped it would all work out with the female sex. Something has to give. Numbers lie.

I reached back for my clothes, but they weren't dry yet. Hattie, in turn, reached back for me, and I obliged. We cuddled some more, and when we were done we fucked again and again and again.

Henri was a good sport about it. He played security guard on the deck of the boat and sat at attention like a solder at roll call. If only the chap could talk. He'd have quite the stories to tell of his master.

When the sun was on its last legs, Hattie and I were like two crossed pretzels. I felt her heart racing a million miles an hour, while mine was now perfect.

"You really are the champ," she said.

"Why thank you," I said.

She punched me, and I let her. I don't remember how many punches that made for the day, but it was definitely a punch fiesta. I expected many more to follow.

She buried her head in my shoulder for a few seconds, and that's when everything changed. I rubbed my eyes just to make sure it was real.

I saw it on the wall of the cabin.

Just three feet away.

A picture.

In a rustic maple frame.

It showed Macho, and the hooker. They looked like they'd just come back from the spa and were trying their hand at fishing. And off to the side was someone else. Somebody I'd never forget.

My dad.

He was in the right-hand corner, almost in profile, fiddling with some wires. I couldn't tell if this was a candid shot, if the photographer had taken my dad by mistake. I sat up on the edge of the bed and examined the picture more closely.

It was fifteen years old, easy. For one, the color was out of date, and two, Macho was wearing a damned fanny pack. His belly was gone, and so was his handlebar mustache. He had an olive tan with a hint of forearm muscle. His olive tee was ripped at the shoulders and converted into a tank top. The hooker wore the shortest shorts I'd ever seen, and she had a nice set of abs to match. Her ass looked A-list, and she must have done a gazillion squats a day to impress her clientele.

My dad didn't fall far behind. He looked chiseled, and he had a five-o'clock shadow on his face. I remembered my mom showing me photos of him growing up, and he hadn't missed a beat in this one. Close-cropped, tight-fitting cotton T-shirt, shorts showcasing all the striations in his quads, and a watch on his wrist. It didn't look like the Seiko from the course, but it didn't matter.

Macho knew my dad.

The asshole really was sending me a message.

"What's wrong?" Hattie said. She sat up behind me and rubbed my shoulders.

I pointed to the photo, and she didn't think anything of it. Then she got up from the bed, pulled it off the wall, and sat back down on the bed, curling her feet up.

"This funny thing?" she said. "Old fucking school."

I showed her who my dad was and told her a little bit about the seaman's history. She nodded at all the right times and used her feminine touch to soothe me at all the others.

"I never knew my asshole boss was a seaman," she said. "But I wouldn't put anything past that man."

I nodded. Macho was full of surprises. I was getting closer, but I needed more. I scanned the picture to see if I recognized any of the geographic features. They were on a dock, and the boat was Macho's boat—albeit much larger than the boat we were on now. It looked much rustier, but also much sturdier. The high seas were a fickle beast. The boat had the letter "M" emblazoned on the back, just like this one had.

The dock in the picture wasn't at Cochiti Lake—there were only runoff ramps here. But the sun and the water seemed eerily New Mexico-esque. I was taking a stab in the dark, but what else was there? I doubted Macho was leading me on a goose chase across the Atlantic to find his ass. Macho wanted me here in New Mexico, plain and simple. He'd started this watch fiasco, and now I'd end it.

"Where's the nearest dock?" I said.

Hattie gave me a puzzled look, then gears started churning in her head.

"I need internet," she said.

I went to my clothes and fished out the Jitterbug. It was a miracle that it'd stayed in my pocket during the fall, and it'd be even more of a miracle if it worked.

I powered it on and pressed the buttons.

Nada. The phone was dead.

Hattie fished her phone out of her jeans and went through the same rigamarole. Her phone wasn't working either. No service.

We sat in silence for a few seconds, and then she told me the plan.

I agreed.

Henri came back in from abovedeck, and I thanked him for his services.

Then I changed into my dry clothes and kept on sleuthing.

24

Hattie lived in a shoebox on Constitution Avenue. Blue socks and green sweatshirts and white tees lined all the floors. Wrenches and dusty books sat on a small coffee table that doubled as a dining table. A queen mattress sat in the east corner of the room with no headboard, footboard, or slats, and a purple bra was crumpled between the sheets.

I loved the ambience of the place, and I felt perfectly at home. While the average hombre lived for the lavish life, I was much more simple. Give me a bed to sleep on and a roof over my head and that's all she wrote. I could make do with just about anything in this world, and that contributed to my examination of all the fine motels across state lines. Pontiac's lessons weren't all bad.

Hattie took off her shoes and threw her phone on her bed, which I realized was just a hand's reach away from the kitchen. She walked over to the fridge and pulled out a pitcher. She offered me water, but I declined. I only drank when I was thirsty, and at the moment I was focused on the task at hand.

Finding the dock.

On the way over, Hattie had given me her opinion on where the dock was. I'd nodded at all the right times and frowned at all the others. I wasn't a geographical wizard by any means, but Hattie was making sense. She'd been to more than her fair share of docks over the years, and her mind was like a sponge. After she'd examined the hue of wood on the dock in the photo, she had a list of contenders in a matter of seconds.

Damn, smart and sexy.

She took a sip of her water, set it down on the counter, then plopped down on the mattress. For a moment I thought she wanted more cardio activities, but then she reached behind where the headboard would have been and pulled out a laptop.

"The motherboard," she said, smiling.

She tapped the keyboard a few times, and the screen lit up like one of those super festive Christmas trees in the town square. I stared at her screen while she typed faster than a hare on the run. Her fingers were on fire, and she had some serious tech game. While I'd adjusted to all the toys on the outside, I still dealt with them like a neanderthal. Slow and steady wins the race.

I sat at one of her dining chairs and analyzed Henri's tactics. He didn't do well in close quarters, and this often resulted in destruction of all property and effects. But this time, he was taking it all in stride. He sat under my feet, staring at one of Hattie's flip-flops. No mouth action at all. Maybe it was Hattie's scent that was putting him at ease, or maybe it was the fact that he was tired as hell.

He'd been through the wringer today and so had I. But a job is a job.

Hattie typed some more, then pointed to her screen.

"Google Street View is the best."

"It's all Greek to me," I said.

"We find this place, you're treating me to some baklava."

"Hell yeah." I was thinking more Canadian maple syrup, but I never turned down the opportunity to enjoy some ethnic sweets with a solid gal.

Hattie told me there were a handful of docks in the vicinity. She'd type each one into Google and then she'd zoom in on the place. It was like I had a front-row seat to all the waterways in New Mexico. She pressed the return key on her computer and she'd get closer and closer.

The first few docks didn't match the architecture of the photo on Macho's boat. Of course, years had gone by since the photo was taken, but the docks themselves likely wouldn't have undergone a massive reconstruction. A paint job or a de-rusting job was more likely. So Hattie and I were looking at shape. Color was negotiable.

"That one," I said. I pointed to a place called Marina Docks.

Hattie shook her head. "Their dock doesn't allow that many boats in season, and it's not wide enough."

I considered a counterargument, but let it pass. I trusted my gut on many things, but nautical dock lengths and widths and diameters weren't on the menu. If Hattie wanted to steer the ship, so be it.

She went through a couple more Google hits, then she found one that was a perennial contender.

The dock was the same color, size, and shape as the one in Macho's photo. I turned the photo in my hands a few times and dissected every angle just to make sure.

It checked out.

Or so I thought.

"The stakes," I said, pointing to the poles that went into the ground. "Wrong ones."

Hattie took the photo from me and analyzed it some more. Then she slapped me across the head with it.

"Those are the mooring poles, man. Different poles for different boats. They're not all equal."

She was right.

Hattie picked up her phone and took a picture of her screen. Then she took another sip of her water and we were ready.

At least I was.

"My clothes haven't fully dried," she said.

She fell on the mattress and started doing snow angels. I was humored by the display, and Henri was too. He started rolling on the ground, mimicking his friend.

Before I could mimic as well, Hattie took her shirt off.

I would have taken my shirt off too, but then there was a knock at the door.

Hattie clutched her legs and curled up on the bed. I went over to the door and looked through the peephole.

A pizza man.

With an eighteen-inch American pie.

The man waited patiently for his services to be rewarded. I didn't let him get off that easy. I waited him out. A con was a con was a con. Hattie hadn't ordered any pizza, and the minute I opened the door, it'd be adios amigo.

Josita could have sent him.

I stared at the dude from the peephole for an eternity, and he stared back. He made no move.

Just bring it, hombre.

Hattie tapped me on the shoulder and wanted a peek. She was fully dressed now and the moment for a quickie had passed faster than you could say quickie.

She looked into the peephole and back at me.

"That's Earl," she said. "He had a TBI a few years back and

always delivers to the wrong place. Lot of college kids in this building who have pizza every night. Assholes."

"Yummy, yummy," I said.

Hattie punched me in the shoulder. "That's not nice, Sherlock."

"Ain't nobody got time for nice when you're on Macho time."

Hattie shook her head.

Henri barked, and just like that we went Macho hunting some more.

25

We found the dock twenty minutes later. It was tucked away in the back of an old warehouse, forming a horseshoe shape. The mooring poles were the same from the photo on Macho's wall, and the boats attached to them were of similar build too. Three crab boats sat there, each one rustier than the next. They looked like they'd been docked there for an eternity, and not a single sign of life existed out on deck.

I walked along with Henri on my left, perfectly heeling, and Hattie on my right, holding my hand. No matter how many experiences I'd had with the female sex, a woman's touch is a woman's touch. No amount of experience could tame the effect it had on me. My traps lowered, my breath slowed, and my head felt so clear. I smiled and felt at peace, despite the constant barrage of conflict that floated in and out of my life like a bout of influenza.

No matter what happened with Macho, I wanted to keep Hattie around for a while. She was really something.

We followed the concrete walkway perpendicular to the

dock and headed toward our destination. We passed the warehouse, which looked eerily similar to the storage place from earlier in the day. The place was just as tall and just as vintage, but the wrought iron doors and rickety boards that doubled as windows gave it some extra flair. No signs of life there either.

We trudged on, Hattie telling me stories about how she'd fixed a tranny in the shop in record time, causing all the boys to lose their moolah. She'd taken them to school, and now she went through the play-by-play of it all. She loved ribbing the crew, and despite her overall affect, she truly was one of the boys. That's why she stayed on when Macho came on. Among other reasons.

I was engrossed in her story and added my two cents' worth here and there. I didn't add anything particularly helpful to the narrative, but sometimes saying something is better than saying nothing at all. When she was winding down, I reminded her that I had to not only find Macho, but I had to get to the society for the speech.

She teased me the rest of the walk on the dock, calling me "Carless fur padre extraordinaire," and I appreciated the creativity.

When we got close to the crab boats, I looked for signs that they could have been Macho's. There wasn't much to go on from the photo, but I figured that a big ole 'M' would be a good place to start, and if that didn't work, maybe an analysis of all the sterns would do it.

The stern in the picture had a yellowish tint. I examined all the boats for a few seconds, but they all looked the same. The sun was down now, and the water was quiet. Even Henri was enjoying the moment, his ears perked up, listening to all of nature's great sounds and not making any in return as he stared off into the distance.

Hattie squeezed my hand.

"When you're done with this mission of yours, we should hang out some more this weekend. You free?"

The million-dollar question. It required a million-dollar answer. If I said I was free, that could communicate desperation on my part and a lack of a social life. If I said I *wasn't* free, then this little bundle of fun would be over with faster than you could say fun. Companionship is a fickle beast.

I decided to stay true to form.

By giving an answer that wasn't quite an answer.

"Old Faithful comes a-calling. Henri wants to see the old geyser."

Hattie looked at Henri, and even he was confused this time. He turned his back to us, curled his ears in both directions, and lay down.

Hattie was quiet for a moment. Then she smiled.

"I figured that, champ. You beat to a different drum, and I like that. If you're ever in town again, I'm not done with you yet."

"Missy, I have no objection."

We both smiled, and then Hattie kissed me. It was a longer kiss than usual, more sensual. Like a goodbye of sorts, even though we still had plenty of time left in the night for sleuthing and other activities.

I took it all in like a boss and returned the favor. We stood there on the dock, locking lips like movie stars. I pulled her closer, and we didn't stop for quite some time. We could have broken the world record, but then Henri barked, and the fun ended.

Life.

He wasn't barking at us, but at something by the front of the warehouse again. He didn't do that well with other dogs, so I didn't think much of it at first. I figured Henri was just marking his territory ahead of an impending showdown in the dark.

"Another stroll?" Hattie said.

I nodded, and we proceeded to walk back in the direction we came. We were within thirty feet of the warehouse when shots were fired.

At us.

Bullets ricocheted off the dock and the crab boats. Henri shrieked, and the shots kept coming. I tackled Hattie to the ground and we took cover behind a lone bush off the dock. I covered her up and wouldn't let go. For a minute, I thought Henri would run away. But he was a trooper, and he lay down next to us, his protective instinct kicking into full gear.

I could hear Hattie's heart beating a million miles an hour. Her palms were sweaty and she was shaking all over. Which wasn't shameful at all. This was the average response to insane trauma.

Fight or flight.

Most chose flight.

I was the fucking opposite.

I loved to fight, and I'd go to my grave loving every inch of it.

Hattie said something that I forget, then a voice came from the direction of the warehouse.

"Come out, you traitors, wherever you are. Always traitors around here."

The voice was male, and the words were undoubtedly slurred. Whoever the dude was, he was having a night of fun, courtesy of some liquid courage.

I peered out from behind the bush. Then ducked back down as another bullet ripped past me into the dock.

Hattie was hyperventilating. I squeezed her hand and

peered up again, a mere half inch this time, and that's when I saw him.

The man of the fucking hour.

Macho.

His handlebar mustache was gone and his belly seemed to have lost an inch or two, but his olive skin was still there. His smug look, too. He was sweating, and he was drunk as fuck. Or high. I couldn't tell which. He was swaying from side to side, firing wildly.

I wasn't much of a gun aficionado, so I couldn't tell what his weapon of choice was. Bottom line, he had a gun and I didn't. His ammo versus my fists.

If I could get to him.

I listened for sirens in the distance. Anything to break the rhythm of the nutjob firing. But all was quiet. Macho had picked the perfect night to break a whole host of laws.

I ducked back down and told Hattie it was Macho. The minute the words left my mouth, she steadied herself and gritted her teeth so hard I thought she would grind them right off. Then she leapt up from our hiding position and screamed at the top of her lungs.

"Paco, what the *fuck*?!"

Macho stopped firing. In his drunken stupor I didn't know if he had seen Hattie, but he'd sure as hell heard her.

I used the temporary stoppage to play hero. I held Hattie back, then walked toward Macho. I had a feeling Macho wouldn't fire at close range. That would have been too easy and would have gone against any master plan he had.

But I was wrong.

I got within ten feet of him, and he pointed the gun right at my face.

"One more step and I blow your brains out," he said.

"What kind of silver is that, tire don?"

Macho was confused by the question.

I pointed to the gun. "The gun, asshole. What kind is it?"

Macho steadied the gun and smiled.

"I run this town, you piece of shit. I can have whatever guns I want. No permits. No restrictions." He waved at the emptiness around us and gloated.

"What about those Cochiti boys?" I said. "They need some firepower for their 'roided testes."

"Who the fuck are you?" Macho said.

Now that I had my quarry, I wasn't going to let him off that easy.

"The heir to the Lord Marvel Seiko watch. You graverobber."

I didn't get into more details. Macho knew the score. He swayed from side to side and fired off another shot. This time he fired it straight out over the water. Then he looked me dead in the eye.

He muttered something that I couldn't make out. He was totally plastered at this point, the alcohol creeping through every crevice of his body. I was waiting for an opening to go to town on his candy ass. One little slip-up, and he was a goner.

"What?" I said.

"Strange lives, strange ends," he said.

The slip-up never came. Before I could say anything else, he faced me directly, and in one fluid motion he pointed the gun at me, closed his left eye, and fired.

He missed me by a mile.

But he hit Hattie right in the forehead.

26

Hattie's brain splattered all over the dock. She'd never fix another tranny again. I wanted to charge Macho, but my feet felt like they were stuck in quicksand. A cloud hung over my head and my eyes were seeing double.

What did you do?

Your fucking games.

Always trying to stick your nose where it doesn't belong.

He should have killed you first.

The demons clung to the synapses of my brain, and my head felt like it was in a vise grip, with nails grinding along the edges of my skull. It wasn't the first time I'd witnessed somebody die in front of me, but all it takes is one time to fuck you up for good. That shit never quite processes right.

It makes you do irrational things.

Like charge at a gunman without a fucking care in the world.

I did a full-on swan dive and connected with his right shoulder. The gun flew out of his hands and into a small patch of grass. I fumbled along the ground trying to get to it first.

Macho was loving every minute of it.

"No more pussy?" he said, mocking me.

He kicked me in the stomach, and I knew that I had my work cut out for me. Macho might have been overweight, but he had that natural strength. The dad bod kind. It couldn't be quantified, and it sure as hell couldn't be underestimated.

I rose up and threw a punch that hit air, and Macho kicked me in the ribs, sending me back to the ground. My vision was all fucked up again, but I didn't care. I wouldn't give up.

For Hattie.

I charged at him again, and he struck me down like a fly.

"I knew leaving the breadcrumbs would be super easy," he said. "The prodigal son returns. For his timepiece."

Macho's sway was almost gone now, and it looked like he'd sobered up in an instant. His eyes were locked on mine, and his teeth were yellower than a canary.

"Daddy made some bad choices, and now the son wants him to stay on the nice list. Oh, boy, what have they done to you all these years? Filling your head with fantasies."

Macho spit on me and picked up the gun. He pointed it at me, then he laughed and put the gun in his pants.

"My fucking watch," I said.

I was slurring my words now. When you get your ass kicked, the body doesn't work the way it's supposed to. I'd been on the giving end most of my career, but I sure as hell had been on the receiving end as well. Every action has a reaction. I was fucked up, but in the fight game the return to glory was always on the horizon.

Once I got my equilibrium back, I'd make my play.

Macho cracked his neck and gave me another kick to the ribs. I was coughing blood, but I didn't mind. Just bring it, hombre.

"We worked on them docks, boy. Your daddy and me.

Ronnie Spikes, the superstar crab man. Always stealing the show. Biggest catch, biggest payout. Everybody wanted to work on his crew. Green makes the world go round. But when you get too big, shit happens, boy."

I got up and threw a jab. It got a piece of Macho's shoulder, but it was only a graze.

Macho slapped my ears.

"Listen, boy. Time for your history lesson. Your daddy didn't share the wealth. New dock. New night. New lay. He had all the bling, and he'd get all the chicks. He was pristine and fit and the whole nine yards, you understand? Untouchable. Hollywood on the water."

I understood, but I couldn't form the words.

"The celebs ain't got nothin' on your daddy though. He'd bang thousands of chicks. His legend was real in the sack. They'd come so loud the waves would get drowned out. Storm or no storm. And they kept coming back for more. They all knew his ass, and they didn't care. A legend's a legend. But then it got too big for him. His true colors shone through."

I got up and tried kicking Macho, but he just sidestepped me and kneed me in the stomach. I went down, but not before I scratched a chunk of his right cheek.

I reached up and tried to dig all my fingers into his skin, but he swatted me away like a fly.

"We'd docked at Homer," he said. "Halibut capital. Tourists up the asshole. The crew went for some pints and your daddy went for some pussy, as always. Rachel Summerdale. Redhead photographer working for *National Geographic*. She wanted the real scoop on how we worked them crabs. Your daddy gave her the real scoop all right. They fucked on the boat. She wanted vanilla, your daddy wanted kink. After so many, missionary don't cut it, sonny."

"Shut the fuck up." I got up again and tried something new.

I got into a Philly shell stance. It was a defensive position where my lead arm lay across my stomach and I tucked my chin. I held my right hand close to my torso so I could cover up and tire my opponent out while he tried to penetrate the shell.

Good luck.

It pissed off everybody in the ring, and they couldn't touch me.

Macho was no different.

He tried kicking me, but I covered up, and his leg was absorbed by the shell.

Then he tried throwing a left hook and a right cross.

Shell.

Shell.

Nada, hombre.

I smiled, and Macho smiled too.

"Your daddy came back with blood on his hands. He was all quiet and shit, but you can't hide on them docks. She was dead. Right in the freezer hold. No inside scoop for her. Your daddy wasn't taking the fall, and no way in hell were we. The Fab Four, boy. That's what we were. Me, your daddy, my sister."

"Smoking fucks up your lungs," I said. "What kind of brother are you?"

Macho smiled. "Josita does have a strong pair of cojones, doesn't she? Though she was a greenhorn at the time, just getting started on the boat. Of course, now it doesn't mean shit because we bettered ourselves. The sea doesn't do it anymore. Not worth dying for those fucking crabs, you feel me?"

Macho threw one of the hardest left hooks ever. I ate the punch and was seeing quadruple. A few more of those and it'd be adios amigo. Macho would stuff me on one of the boats, regardless of ownership.

"The human soul can forgive, but can never forget," he

said. "Your daddy threatened to destroy us. He started seeing shit in his sleep, and blabbing to the old-timers in all the pubs. He had a mouth on him and he was saying all the wrong lines. Self-preservation is a beautiful thing. Take the damned Seiko. That watch worked wonders on your ass."

"How did you get it?" I said.

"Boy, it's a replica. But your ass fell for it, hook, line, and sinker. Lure the champ and watch him follow the trail. You have a reputation for doing some brazen things, sonny. Just like your daddy. The worldly nomad. New city, new day. Not hard to learn a thing or two about big ole Gedrin. You were coming to this town, and we were fucking ready for you."

I threw a punch, and this time I connected. Macho rubbed his cheek and I could see it starting to swell.

Macho mocked me.

"That all you got, champ?"

It sure seemed like it, but a fighter never quits. Maybe it's part pride or maybe it's part dilapidation of brain cells, but you never quit till the bell rings.

I faked a jab, and threw a teep.

This caught Macho off guard, and unlike my first kick, this one caused Macho to fall to his knees. I kicked him again, this time in the face, and he keeled over.

When I went for a third, he caught my ankle, and bit down on it.

There are no rules in the street fight game.

I writhed in pain, and Macho punched me in the ribs again and again. He got back up to his feet and starting throwing elbows too.

"Moolah is a beautiful thing too, boy. I have so much of it these days, but you can never have enough for the ladies in your life. Am I right?"

Macho threw some more combos, but I managed to time

my head movement perfectly. With each throw, I slipped and bobbed and weaved and he missed and hit grass. He was tiring out, and I had him right where I needed him.

In every fight, there's a turn-of-the-tide moment. Some mistake or overcalculation happens that shifts everything. The aggressor becomes defensive, and the defensive person becomes the aggressor.

It's a comeback. Plain and simple. The crowd ate that shit up.

Macho used his hands and pinned my stomach to the grass. Then he lifted his knees up to deliver a double knee strike. The highlight blow.

But the tide turneth.

I elbowed him right in the face, and he collapsed off of me. Then I went to town on him for so many minutes that I couldn't believe Macho was still breathing. The tire don had a bunch of fucking heart.

I stood over him and spit on his face.

He smiled, his lips all crooked and smashed.

"Don't forget the fourth," he said. "Your daddy won't forget it."

I couldn't tell if Macho was on his last legs, or if he was just trying to get a rise out of me so I could lower my guard.

He must have sensed my confusion because he cleared his throat.

"The Fab Four, boy. Get the picture?"

He enunciated "picture," extra long and hard, and my mind ran through hoops with what little stores I had left.

The picture.

The four.

The dock.

Yes.

The hooker. Macho. My dad.

I couldn't think of any other pictures, but I didn't have to. It took me a few more seconds, then it came to me.

The hooker didn't count. But there was another person in that picture. I'd paid him no attention before because he was on the boat, not looking at the camera.

But he was there.

The fourth in the Fab Four.

And he was somebody I had met before.

I looked over at Macho, and he had snot coming out of his nose with pools of blood. I knocked him out for good and called Henri.

I had some unfinished business, but so did he.

He was curled up by Hattie's body, crying.

I stayed with him for a few minutes, slowly rubbing the top of his head. I told him everything would be okay and that revenge is a dish best served cold.

Stone cold.

27

There weren't any more tee times at Rainmaker Golf Club. Which was great for me because I wasn't there to play another round. The parking lot was deserted, but I knew that there was still life out on the course. The trees whistled in the distance, and the sprinklers came to life.

I told Henri to "get it" and he left my side and sprinted onto one of the fairways. I had no idea which hole we were on, but soon enough it wouldn't mean shit.

Henri had a plethora of talents, and one of them was tracking humans. Once he found his target, he'd let out three barks, and he'd be rewarded with heaps of praise. He'd developed the skill well before I'd rescued him from his serial killer mama, but I'd never put it to use. I enjoyed tricks and companionship more than olfactory skills. In other words, I picked and chose my spots with my best friend.

Like now.

Henri barked three times, and I smiled.

I walked calmly through the darkness. The lights of the clubhouse were shining the way, but I was in no rush to school my quarry. The slower the better. It'd make more of an impact that way.

When I got within a few feet, Henri barked three times again, louder this time. He returned to my side, and I gave him some treats.

Then I addressed the shadows.

"Fess up or you fucking die."

There was a long pause, then the landscaper with the turtle's nest stepped off his cart and put his hands up.

"*Nie, mow*," the conman said.

He had his hands up in surrender, but I knew the score. I wouldn't be played any longer.

The landscaper was the fourth man from the picture on Macho's wall. He'd been on Macho's boat back in the day, and he'd known my dad. The asshole thought he could keep the con going. But the jig was up.

"Fess up or you die," I said again.

The landscaper looked me up and down like I had the plague. Then I caught a corner of his lip curling upward. The lights from the clubhouse were at my back, but they weren't illuminating the rest of his shitty face.

"Sure took you long enough, kiddo," he said. "Stupid as fuck, just like your old man."

He backpedaled to his cart and pulled out a shovel. It was a gargantuan shovel, perfect for all the turtle nests in the world. He twirled it in his hands, but made no move with it.

He wanted to play it slow.

I had no problem with that. My body was still healing from my previous activities in the great state of New Mexico, and the more time he gave me, the more time I had to formulate my plan. Aside from kicking his candy ass to oblivion, I wanted to make sure he spilled real good.

"Tell me about them crabs," I said.

The landscaper faked a shot with the shovel, pulled back, and laughed.

"Crabs aren't for everyone, kiddo. Some people have it in them. They get on them boats and when those waves come, they don't shit their pants. Their stomach is harder than Valyrian steel. Greenhorn or no greenhorn, they don't back down. And they keep coming back for more. Your old man was like that."

The landscaper swung the shovel at my head, but I slipped it. He started walking in circles, feigning like he was gonna hit me, but pulling off at the last second and laughing his ass off. He had a maniacal laugh, one that I'd heard many times over the years.

Good things seldom follow such laughs.

"But he was a fucking rapist," the landscaper said. "He did that girl for no reason. Left her to die on that boat because she wouldn't tie his ass up, stick an apple in his mouth, and spank him."

"Shut it," I said.

I half-charged him, and slipped another shovel shot. I got him with a jab, and the landscaper touched his nose and wiped off some of the blood.

"Not bad," he said. "Still a pussy shot, but not bad."

He hoisted the shovel on his shoulder and continued prose-lytizing like a warden on the prison yard.

"Paco and Josita didn't take too kindly to rape ruining their livelihood on the docks, so evaporation was the name of the game. The girl's body had to go, and go it did. The whole thing was memory-holed. Or would have been, but your old man couldn't let it go. Lotta demons inside that one. A tortured soul who wanted to spend life behind bars where he belonged. How noble of him."

The landscaper hoisted the shovel on his other shoulder,

and this time the light from the clubhouse hit just the right angle and I saw the strain under his eyelids. He was giving his two cents' worth, but Father Time plays no favorites.

"He got batshit crazier with each job," he said. "He'd check every compartment of the boat twenty times and he'd rewrite the same paperwork over and over again. When we stopped at the local watering holes he'd share missing person stories, with names omitted of course. He was at the end of his lead. For him, and for us."

"Where is he," I said. It was a question, but it came out more like a statement.

"Sonny, your old man is with the crabs where he belongs."

I threw a right hook, but the landscaper got me with the shovel and I staggered back. He hit me in the left kneecap, and I buckled to the ground like putty.

I willed my body up, but there was nothing doing. My eyes were seeing floaters and my ears were ringing. I looked around for Henri and couldn't find him.

The landscaper knew I was losing this one, so he went to town on my kneecap. I bit the inside of my cheeks and writhed in pain. My head was pounding, but I had to move.

I pushed off with my left palm, but gravity is gravity, hombre. I couldn't put any pressure on it. The landscaper stepped on my wrist, and I told him to go fuck himself in several languages.

"The loran giveth and taketh away," he said. "Got it? Long-range navigation system. It fueled the seas back in the day. None of this GPS shit they have now. The transmitter stations sat on all the major shipping lanes and they sent pulses of energy out on the water faster than the speed of light. The loran gear on the boat would receive the signal, and based off that shore station signal, you'd be able to determine a line and where the hell you were, sonny."

He stepped harder on my wrist, and I could feel myself losing consciousness.

"But the line is only as good as the receiver at the controls. I was always the receiver, and you reach your limit sometimes. Your old man confessed to the girl's family. When we went back to Homer. He wrote a letter, tucked it away in a box, and dropped it off at their front step. That's the long and short of it. Your old man ruining us all in one fell swoop. So when it was just me and him on the boat, I did the honors. I fucked with the signals."

I mustered up every last fiber of my being and bit the landscaper's leg. His foot left my wrist faster than you could say hola. I hobbled back up and tried another dive, but my track record was too good from earlier today. I was bound to misfire epically, and that's exactly what happened.

The landscaper moved out of the way, and I crashed into his cart.

I saw quintuple landscapers, and they weren't Polish at all.

He smiled. "I left his raping ass out on that boat and sent a signal back to the transmitter. I would have left it at that. Bogus signal, bogus navigation back. Your old man couldn't operate the boat even if you hit him in the goddamned head with all the pictures. He was a crab catcher, nothing more. But all's fair in love and war."

He smiled again. "I slit his throat and wiped his blood with one of his fucking watches."

I bounced back up and threw some of the best combinations I've ever thrown. Adrenaline is a beautiful thing. But learning my dad was murdered at sea probably played a role as well. I unloaded on the fucking landscaper and the shovel fell from his hands.

I picked it up, and I needed no pictures.

It was my turn to smile.

"*Nie, mow,*" I said.

I went to town on his kneecaps, and the landscaper's cries could be heard all the way back at Cochiti Lake.

"Like father, like son," he spit out. "When the world gets wind of this, you're done. Paco will make sure of it. Your brand is fucked."

I spit on his face.

"My brand's been fucked a long time ago, hombre."

I took the shovel and I made a Picasso with his face. I killed a murderer, and when it was done I saw my mom again. The synapses were speaking.

She was proud, but I felt nada.

I wondered whether I really was like my old man. A charismatic ladies' man who doubled as a sociopath.

Before I could analyze the nuances in my brain, everything went black.

28

I woke up on Macho's boat. I was tied to a chair on deck, and the thugs from the water were back. The bodybuilder was gone, but the muscle tee hombres sat off to one side, smiling.

It was dark on the water, and if it wasn't for the light on deck the vibe would have definitely resembled the latest horror flick. I played with the ropes behind my wrists, but nothing doing.

I would have tried all day, but Josita had other plans. She stepped past my right shoulder and slapped the shit out of me. My face started to swell like a watermelon. When I looked down at her hands I saw she had brass knucks. Oh, the irony. I'd used them on more than one occasion and was intimately familiar with the power they had.

Sometimes the circumstances call for nothing less.

"Pendejo, you don't listen," she said.

She walked right in front of me and threw a hard right at my jaw.

I was numb.

But not out.

I closed my eyes and clenched my abs. If I got through this next segment of the proceedings, I could make a move.

Josita unloaded on me.

Hard rights and lefts to my chest and stomach and shoulders.

I absorbed all the impacts, and when she was done I still had my comedic touch.

"Tengo problemas," I said.

She flared her nostrils like a rhinoceros and held up her phone.

"I'll make this real easy, gringo. I want damages. For all the shit you caused since you've arrived in this place. Wire all your money into my account, and we'll call it even. Fair deal to me."

She whipped me with the phone, then pulled back.

"Oh, gringo. And one more thing. I get your perro too."

She nodded to the muscle tee hombres and they walked below deck for a moment and came back out with a very large metal crate.

Henri was inside, clawing at the bars, trying to get the hell out of Dodge. He had way more energy than usual, so I gathered that they'd hopped him up on some non-doggie pills.

I gave Josita and her crew the death stare.

Pride cometh before the fall.

Come, kitty kitty.

Your candy asses are mine.

I smiled, and Josita didn't take too kindly to my bravado. She took a knife out of her pocket and slit my wrist. Blood gushed onto the deck, but I'd had worse.

Just bring it.

I licked some of my blood and spit at Josita.

She gave a smile of her own and dug her nails into my wrist.

"Hijo de puta," she said. "You think you have all the cojones like your stupid father?"

She laughed like a true heel and shoved the phone back in my ear.

"Dinero, gringo. Now."

She asked me for the number, and I gave it to her.

One ring.

Two rings.

Three.

The asshole was busy, but that wasn't a surprise.

On the fourth ring, Sims picked up.

"Sims," he said.

I cleared my throat and said exactly what needed to be said under such exigent circumstances.

"Free the pancakes!" I shouted.

The line went dead.

Josita took out her gun and shoved it in my mouth.

"Gringo, your fun in the sun ends here."

She turned and fired into Henri's cage.

I heard a low whimper...

And then nothing.

Summoning every ounce of strength I had left in me, I stood up in the chair and knocked Josita down. The muscle tee hombres charged me, but I knocked them down too. I was like a spinning axe taking everybody to school.

One of the legs of the chair loosened, and I was able to get one leg free. Then my other one. I got rid of the rest of the ropes and slammed the chair down on Josita's face. Then I went to town on the other hombres.

I took my time.

They were tough motherfuckers.

When I was done, I went to Henri's cage.

"One more step, gringo, and I put it in your brain."

Josita's face was lopsided, but she was even tougher than the hombres. I had two options.

Option A.

Go out on my sword.

Option B.

Give the command.

I smiled.

"Matala," I said.

I kicked the crate, and Henri sprang out faster than a junkie on speed. He thrashed Josita's arms like she was a rag doll and wouldn't let go till I gave the release command.

I didn't.

Henri had dodged that bullet like a boss. It had lodged in the crate. And now he was showcasing all his talents like a best friend would.

I tossed the thugs in the water and returned to my quarry.

"Not so fast," a voice said.

I turned to see Macho, limping on one leg, gun in hand.

Ah, the last of the Mohicans.

He pointed it straight at my face.

I didn't even flinch.

"Henri, matalo."

Henri released his hold on Josita and used his jaws on Macho.

As Macho writhed in pain, I took his gun and pistol-whipped Josita for good measure.

Then I got my Jitterbug out. It was working again, despite all the hoopla of the evening. I called Fester and told him it was time to stick it to his ex-lover and unretire.

29

I was seven minutes late for my keynote speech. The Dobermans for Life Society was a stalwart all across America. They had banquets, trainings, agility competitions, and more. Their members loved the breed and did everything in their power to ensure that the breed was well taken care of and promoted in dog owner circles. After all, being a fur parent was a lot of responsibility, and the more training and support one received, the better off he or she would be.

My involvement was a product of happenstance. The president of the society had reached out to Sims, and then Sims had reached out to me, but my Jitterbug hadn't been working for a stretch after my visit to Horseshoe Bend. After a few weeks of missed connections, I finally fixed my technological marvel and got the call.

They wanted me to give a speech on how much the breed meant to me and how Henri came into my life. Upon hearing that, I had every intention of spilling the goods in certain parts and being coy in others. I'd agreed to the speech in record time. Henri was my world. The rascal filled it with loads of fun, and he was a quick learner. The more trouble I got myself into, the more trouble Henri got into. He always stood by my side, not asking any questions. He could dodge bullets and maul people on command, and he was just as much a badass as his second owner in life.

Henri wasn't going anywhere, and neither was I.

So I was relieved that I made it to the venue in the end. Sims had hooked me up with a suit to replace the blood-stained ensemble I was wearing. He even brought a brush for Henri's coat. We both had to look solid in front of the members.

I walked to the entrance of the banquet hall, and the name-checker didn't even ask for credentials. He just motioned me inside and petted Henri on the way in.

If the outside was lax, the inside was even more so. Scores of Dobermans were running around the main ballroom in total bliss. Their owners would chastise them here and there, but the Dobermans had been given free rein over the premises. They had all the play partners in the world.

Henri tugged at his leash and whined. He wanted to join the fun. A few months ago I would have hesitated; Henri didn't play nice with others, and he was an absolute wild card. But now, Henri was muy bueno.

I told him to play nice, and I let him off leash. He sprinted to the nearest Doberman, and a smelling contest began. Henri passed the test, and off he went.

He was a natural.

"What a beautiful animal," Fester said.

I turned, and Fester was all smiles. He wasn't suited up for the occasion, but he was in full brass uniform.

"The best of the best," I said.

"Hell of a job out there, Gedrin. You brought down one of the biggest drug operations in all of the southwest. Some catch for an unretiree."

"That's how I roll," I said.

Fester nodded. "And to think that asshole Paco was at the head of it all. The tires didn't do it for his rich ass. Revenge is a dish best served cold, my friend. Remember that for the rest of your life."

"It's music to my ears."

"He won't go quietly though," Fester said. "The tire shops are gonna take a hit with the bad press, but he's got a stockpile of cash. Top lawyers in the business. You may be called to testify at some point. So don't stray too far from these parts."

"I'll be in Old Faithful," I said.

"Hell of a place," Fester said.

"Indeed. How'd Josita make out?"

Fester shook his head. "That bitch lawyered up the minute the patrol arrived on scene. Hell, they're both going down for the drugs. That's a slam dunk. The murder of the girl, that's another matter."

"It's all Macho to me."

Fester smiled. "You're something else, you know that?"

He gave me a fist bump, and just like that Fester was gone. Justice would be served, in some fashion. Of course, there was no bringing Hattie back or the landscaper or the myriad of others that were below ground because of the events that had been put in motion by that asshole Macho.

Life was never smooth, but one thing was constant: When something didn't sit right with me, I never let it be. I had to make it right. Till the day I died, that ethos would stay in my blood. Where there was trouble, I would run toward it. I didn't play. Whether it was the Machos or the Jukos or the Zemuns of the world, whenever things seemed off-kilter, I would set it straight.

I was the champ, but I was also the sleuth. An amateur one, but better than nothing, hombre.

I took in the dogs having a blast and the stage and the tables that were set out for all the members. They were sparsely laid out, and there were metal covers on all the tables to minimize the effect of canine paws and nails. It was unworkable, but so be it.

Somebody rang a cowbell, and the noise must have penetrated all the canine ears, because they started running back toward their owners.

Henri didn't follow the crowd. He was laid out on the other side of the ballroom, completely spent.

I called his name twice, and he looked at me like I had the plague.

I took a venison treat out of my suit pocket and called his name again. The third time was the charm, and I rewarded my pal.

I took the stage and gave a knockout speech. I was proud of myself. I used no notes and I never mentioned pancakes. Henri performed some tricks for the masses, and we got a round of applause that rivaled even the crowds in the boxing ring.

Then they opened up the floor for questions. The members wanted to know what I fed Henri, how many hours of exercise he got per day, and what my training regimen was. I figured it was the perfect opportunity for a soundbite, so I gave them one.

"A day in the life of Henri is a day in the life of Gedrin. He follows me everywhere and is a true nomad like his furrever parent. He's a badass on many levels."

The crowd ate it up, and the dinner started. Sea bass and sprouts and rice and some other delicacy that I couldn't quite figure out. I wasn't that hungry, so I gave it all to Henri. I told him to wait, and I got up to go to the pisser.

Right before I reached the doors, I saw him.

Sims.

"You look like shit," he said.

"Good evening, counselor," I said.

Sims looked like a million bucks, as always. He'd hooked me up with a suit, but his always had to be better. Fine Italian fabrics that would make all of Europe proud. That's how he rolled.

"Every time you try and relax there's something I have to fix," he said.

"Good agents are worth their price in gold."

Sims smiled. "How quick can you make weight?"

Getting into the ring was the last thing on my mind, but I knew where this was going.

"No comprendo," I said.

Sims took an envelope out of his pocket, rubbed his hands along the edges, opened it, and handed it to me.

"I got you a title shot. HBO outbid the rest."

I skipped over the legalese and went straight to the place where all fighters looked: the numbers. Sims had come through, big-time. So many zeros I could buy a million Jitterbugs and still have enough for a million more.

But I wasn't letting Sims get off that easy.

"I'm not signing shit until I eat some pancakes. Where's the best spot around here?"

Sims's face got red for a moment, and I could see the gears turning in his head. He couldn't fail his superstar client.

He caved.

"Asshole," he said. "I should have swung a deal for the undercard. Let's get outta here."

I smiled and called Henri.

30

Old Faithful is one of about five hundred geysers in Yellowstone National Park. It was discovered circa 1870 by the Washburn Expedition, and ever since it's been a popular site for tourists, passersby, and the world alike.

The geyser has erupted more than a million times since its inception, and with each eruption reaching at least one hundred fifty feet high and lasting for several minutes, it's no surprise that the place still stands supreme as one of Earth's geographical marvels.

I had it on my bucket list for other reasons. Namely, it was just damned cool and unpredictable. Exactly when it would erupt each day was a mystery that baffled even the best scientists in the world. They came close to figuring it all out, but they still couldn't quite crack the code.

Maybe Henri could do it. He sat at my side now, tilting his head both ways at the beautiful display of nature. We'd left New Mexico the previous night, and this morning we'd made it to our next item on the list.

Life was meant to be lived to the fullest. Every part of the world was meant to be explored completely and without shame. If I had my way, I'd explore every nook and cranny of this world, and I'd build a scrapbook of tales and memories.

As I stared out at the crowds surrounding the geyser, I wondered what it would be like to have my dad here with me. I pictured him spinning yarns and showcasing his brawn and cracking jokes that only he'd understand. But the more the images played in my head, the more I had to compartmentalize them from the truth.

My dad was a rapist, and he got killed by a landscaper. He never had his day in the court of law or in the court of public opinion. He was an asterisk, relegated to figments of the imagination and old legends from the masters of the sea. He had the benefit of the doubt because the world didn't know the truth of his activities.

They couldn't handle the truth.

But I fucking could. I'd sleep well at night knowing that while I shared some of the same gene pool as Papa Gedrin, I was my own man.

And I'd keep on kicking.

Life is full of surprises, but the power is in the journey. Learning, loving, living. I had no idea how many brain cells I had left, and I didn't care. I'd keep kicking ass till I ran out.

I smiled as the geyser erupted again. Then I closed my eyes and wondered where I'd go next. Maybe I'd go east and explore Manhattan. Maybe I'd go south to Mexico and test out my Spanish. Alaska sounded intriguing too. The options are endless. The world is my oyster.

Of course, I'd fight for the title. I still hadn't signed the contract yet, but Sims would get his way. And I would get mine. My camp was wherever the hell I wanted it to be.

Since I was a nomad, my next camp was a complete wild card.

I loved it that way.

I took one last look at the geyser, then walked back to the street. One thing popped into my head, and I couldn't get rid of it. I took out my phone and ordered a ride.

A self-driving one.

Henri and I had to get used to the apparatus.

AUTHOR'S NOTE

Thanks for reading! I hope you enjoyed the Gedrin universe just as much as I enjoyed writing it. I would greatly appreciate it if you would leave a review on Amazon. Reviews allow more readers to find Gedrin, and this ultimately allows me to keep writing stories that I hope will leave an indelible footprint in our literary world.

—Greg

ACKNOWLEDGMENTS

Thank you to my team. Writing may be a solitary endeavor, but publishing is certainly a collective one. Thank you to my beta readers Bailee Myers and Miranda Niles. Your early insights really helped whip Gedrin into shape.

Thank you to my editor David Gatewood for making my prose shine. Thank you to my proofreader Donna Rich for snagging those pesky typos. Thank you to my cover designers at Deranged Doctor Design. I'm blown away by all the Gedrin covers and this one is no different.

And of course thank you to all those who have shaped my writing indirectly in some way. It's impossible to mention everybody here, but y'all know who you are.

ALSO BY GREG GOUNTANIS

SNEAK PEEK THE
JOBBER (GEDRIN #4)

I was smitten for the umpteenth time. Henri was my witness. When you rescue a Doberman from his old serial killer jefe, he tends to take sides.

We were at the San Antonio Riverwalk on a sweaty August morning. I wanted to escape training camp for my next fight and Henri wanted to make friends with the ducks. He tugged on his leash, got down on all fours, and inched his nose toward the edge of the water. The ducks played hard to get, but knowing Henri, he had a backup plan. If perchance the ducks quacked in his direction, Henri would join them. He was a natural swimmer and a natural boss. He'd lead the pack downstream, and I'd be hyperventilating every step of the way.

Unfortunately, I didn't possess any snorkeling game, and I was several fries short of a happy meal when it came to floating, diving, plunging, and the like. I gripped Henri's leash so tight it should have complained. He kept his gaze on the ducks, so I tried another tack.

"Let's go get some food," I said.

Henri ate it up.

He stood ramrod straight like a soldier at roll call and gazed into my eyes so long I felt bad for making him wait. I rummaged in my pocket and gave him the lone remaining duck biscuit left.

"I'll stock up on the way home, don't worry."

Henri gazed at me less enthusiastically this time and we continued down the riverwalk. We'd been at it for the last fifteen minutes, and I was feeling thirsty.

I was approaching one of the food and drink stands when I saw her.

No more than twenty paces in front of me. Five-foot-five, a shade over one hundred twenty pounds, chiseled frame, with beige Ray-Bans. She wore a gray pair of joggers, a black tee with words I couldn't quite place, and white trainers. Her brunette locks were pulled back in a short ponytail, and she moved with a purpose.

I paid for my water bottle and took Henri in her direction. I didn't want to make it obvious that I was enamored by her trainers so I held back a few paces and examined the foliage on the path. The joggers girl seemed lost in thought. She was examining the water and the pedestrian bridges in the distance. At one point she stopped by a bench, tied her shoes with one hand, stretched out her hamstrings and kept going. Looking, smiling, closing her eyes, and repeating. It went like that for several minutes. In an age when the average woman was tethered to her fruit phone waiting for all the small boxes to pop up and ping, it was refreshing to see a woman appreciate the great outdoors.

Henri got sick of my analysis, so he rolled on his back and curled his paws up in a fetal position. I smiled and rubbed him fully. I reached for a treat, but then remembered I needed to get him some more. My mind did that sometimes. Forgetfulness was a thing in the fight game.

I tugged on Henri's leash and we kept walking in the direction of the joggers girl. She was a solid thirty paces in front, and the path was starting to fill up with more tourists. The sun was getting heavier so I had some water and then trudged on. I had no idea what I would say if I eventually crossed paths with her and made a comment about her trainers. I tended to go with the flow when it came to male-female interactions. Truth be told, my record with the female sex was the greatest parabola of all time. I gained and lost significant others like a bout of influenza. Maybe it had to do with the fact that I broke people's skulls for a living, or that I was a nomad in a new motel in a new state of the union the majority of the time.

If that wasn't it, then maybe it was the fact that I'd done twelve years for a murder I didn't commit and came damned close to getting a three-drug cocktail that would have stopped my heart forever before I was sprung on a technicality.

That's why spontaneity is such a beautiful thing. If the joggers girl wanted to talk, then I'd talk. If not, then so be it. Henri would get some pets and we'd be on our way. Complicating matters was that I was a celebrity of sorts. I tried to lay low because of all the gawkers and media hombres, yet I was ever the optimist with each new interaction. Perhaps things would click in the Lone Star State and I'd meet a mesmerizing nomad who had a thirst for more.

Till then, I'd take my crookeds with the straights.

The joggers girl was ten feet away, turning toward one of the pedestrian bridges. Perhaps the real reason I wanted to chat with her was because I could have sworn I'd met her before. I couldn't quite place it, but I knew deep down that we'd crossed paths at some point, and I needed to assuage my curiosity.

Ten seconds later, everything changed.

The joggers girl walked up the bridge, and when she got about halfway, she was surrounded by a bunch of goons. Three in front, and three from behind. If I had to make a hypothesis, they were a mini bling ring going up and down the riverwalk taking shit off all the tourists. Hard-ass wannabes who needed to be put in their place.

I loosened my grip on Henri's leash and clenched my right fist. I was playing all the scenarios in my head, and they all involved a heavy dose of carnage inflicted by me upon the wannabes. I could take them all out in about eleven seconds flat if I was efficient. If I was less than efficient, it'd take me about thirteen seconds, and if I was having a bad day, it'd take me about twenty seconds, and by then my actions would grab the attention of more passersby, deterring the wannabes from coming back for more.

My plan was to keep it relatively civilized. I'd throw a few over the water, break a couple noses and ribs, and I'd let the last hombre run back home to Mama. The fight game was muy bueno.

I smiled as the violent thoughts swirled in my head.

But none of it mattered.

The joggers girl did all the work for me. One of the wannabes stepped toward her and she roundhouse kicked him to the face. The dude was seeing a plethora of sheep. Then she slipped a wobbly punch and left hooked another dude into next week. One wannabe ran off, and the three on the other side of the bridge all charged at her in a triangular formation. Strength in numbers. Hell no. The joggers girl caught one dude in a chokehold and put him to sleep in seconds. Then she delivered a crisp uppercut to one of the other dudes. The third got such a hard liver shot I could see his stomach shaking for an eternity. There was no way he'd ever be able to consume another sip of alcohol.

She was more than efficient. It took her ten seconds to dispatch all the wannabes. I kept count in my head. When it was all done, she dusted off her black tee and picked her phone up off the ground. She dusted that off too and put it back in her pocket. I could see some tourists farther down the walkway clapping, but the joggers girl ignored them.

I'd seen enough, and apparently so had Henri. He pulled me onto the bridge and ran up to the woman, wagging his tail back and forth.

The joggers girl snapped out of it and smiled.

"So cute," she said, rubbing Henri's whiskers.

I was smitten.

"He's drawn to badass women," I said.

She laughed, and I knew right then and there I'd definitely met her before.

"Lance Gedrin," I said, putting my hand out.

She raised her eyebrows. "We still do that nowadays?" She lifted her elbow and made like she was gonna give me an elbow dab.

I pulled my hand back and moved for an elbow dab too, but she stopped me at the last second.

"Just fucking with you, Gedrin," she said.

She shook my hand.

"How could I miss the heavyweight champ of the world checking me out and using his dog as a chick magnet?"

I usually had a witty reply to everything, but sometimes you gotta fall on your sword.

"Preach, mystery woman," I said.

She smiled.

"Hayley Devin, but you know that already."

It all clicked.

I knew we'd met before.

Hayley Devin was the former UFC flyweight champion of the world. I'd seen her achieve some of the most brutal knockouts in the octagon. She dribbled people's heads off the cage, and many of her foes were too fucked up to ever fight again. I'd never met her in person, but there's an intimacy on the television screen that never goes away.

"Imagine that," I said. "Two champs on the same bridge at the same time in the Lone Star State."

"Does that work with all the girls?"

"Just the champs," I said.

Devin gave me a playful push, then she petted Henri again.

"What brings you out here?"

"I'm dodging camp and making my way to the Sand Dunes to sled. They have some really high peaks in Colorado." I told her about the bucket list that I'd established since I'd gotten out of the joint and how I wanted to hit up new spots as much as I could.

"The Dunes suck, but dodging camp, I dig that."

I never changed an item on my list for anybody, so I knew right then and there that it'd be just me and Henri on the slopes.

"And what brings you out here, ass kicker?" I said.

Devin rolled her eyes. "Was in Austin taking in the sights, but then I have this damned presser for my next fight tonight in this rickety gym down here in San Antonio, so I came a little early. I'm with a smaller promotion since the big boys dropped me."

"The struggle is real," I said. "Good left hook by the way."

"I learned from the best."

We shared a laugh, but it didn't last long.

Devin got a text on her phone and everything changed.

GET The Jobber Now on Amazon

JOIN GREG'S NEWSLETTER

For the latest updates on Greg's writing, sign up for his newsletter at: https://dashboard.mailerlite.com/forms/1415379/150624884207126495/share

ABOUT THE AUTHOR

Greg Gountanis writes mysteries and thrillers filled with a lot of action, wit, and courtroom drama. When he's not writing, he's lawyering. For over a decade, Greg's worked as a public defender in Chicago.

Get the latest news on Greg's books at www.greggountanis.com and on social media.

f facebook.com/GregGountanisAuthor

a amazon.com/stores/author/B08P1C58RR

▶ youtube.com/greggountanis